# Nomad

ISBN: 1940597919
ISBN-13: 9781940597911

# Nomad

## Operation Overwatch
### The Mark Mitchell Chronicles
Travis Wright
Edited by Jenny Neyman
Cover design or artwork by Melanie Noblin

Be tough when you feel weak. Be courageous when you are afraid. Be humble when you are triumphant. Never give up, even when it feels like all hope is lost, and shoot truer than your enemies.

# Prologue

The Sangin area of northeastern Helmand Province in Afghanistan is monitored by men and women on the ground, as well as drones in the sky and satellites hundreds of miles above the Earth. The full might of the U.S. military and coalition forces do their best to police and protect the local populace while fending off the Taliban and Al-Qaeda extremists wreaking havoc in the country. Special Forces operators and private contractors work behind the scenes with and without the aid of agencies having no names or acronyms.

The different sects of the region have been at war with outsiders and each other for thousands of years. They are no strangers to violence or death. Since before Christ, dozens of empires have ruled the country and influenced the culture now flourishing there. Afghanistan has always been strategically significant, not only for military purposes, but the land has served as a gateway to India. Trade routes from the Mediterranean to China converged through the heart of the land over the centuries. The societies being mainly Sunni Islam, belong to different rural tribes. Getting to know the locals and trying to gain some semblance of trust is always the first step in any circumstance, whether it's for profit, protection or control.

The lush river valley in southern Helmand is another hotspot known to be an area for global Islamic extremist organizations to smuggle drugs, weapons and fighters into and out of the country. Subsistence farming provides a food source for the population, but the main source of income for the 1.4 million inhabitants are the poppy fields which supply 75 percent of the world's opium and is converted into drugs such as heroin, morphine and codeine. This is possible with the help of irrigation canals fed from the hydro-electric dam, Grishk, built by the U.S. in the 1960s and a main reason for the influx of Taliban and Al-Qaeda forces into the region. The mountains provide a natural place for the worldwide terror organizations to hide and train while taking advantage of the lucrative opium trade that aids them in financing missions against their enemies within the country and abroad.

The shark-finned ridges of the Hindu Kush Mountains in the Himalayan range, towering above luxuriant valleys of Panjshir and Bayman with their daunting presence, hold some of the most hostile and unforgiving places on the planet. They pierce the sky like gigantic spearheads frozen in place from times as old as Alexander the Great.

Most roads in the country are dirt and about a third are only accessible part of the year, causing U.S. and coalition troops to utilize helicopters as their main mode of transportation. Humvees, 5-ton trucks and other military vehicles can only reach some parts of the mountainous areas, so dangerous foot patrols have to be implemented, as well.

# Chapter One

**Helmand Province, Afghanistan**
**Sangin area, above the "Fish Tank"**
**Monday, October 6th, 1103 Hours**

"Here we go again! Those Marines down there are in the thick of it," advised Mark's spotter and constant reminder of why he'd left the Corps in the first place. In his mid 40s, he was a nice enough older guy from Brooklyn but acted like he was still on active duty, sporting the same jarhead haircut he'd worn for years. He looked to be in good shape but had a pockmarked face from bad acne in his younger years. He hung out with the Marines on base and told war stories which got more intense with each retelling, like a fish tale. The younger Marines ate it up. He was always smiling, hence the nickname "Happy."

"Nothing we can do to help them right now without giving away our position. And besides, they're out of range even for the .50 cal." Mark replied. He wanted to help his fellow Marines in the worst way but he had orders to follow and shouldn't — no — couldn't piss off the colonel *again*.

"Can't we at least call in artillery on the insurgent position, forthwith?" Happy asked, handing Mark a notepad with grid coordinates.

"Yeah, let me see what I can do," Mark muttered reluctantly as he grabbed the radio handset while spitting out another sunflower seed shell. "Double Tap, this is Deadeye, over."

"This is Double Tap, go ahead with y'alls traffic, over," drawled a sweet southern voice, sounding like soft country music in Mark's ear. Mark found it harder and harder to restrain himself when he was off duty with the owner of that voice.

"Hey Sandy...uh, I mean Double Tap. We have a platoon of Darkhorse Marines in contact in the valley below. They're pinned down and meeting heavy resistance from what appears to be a sizable insurgent force. We're requesting some arty to help 'em out, over."

"Request denied, you boys better stay on mission," barked Col. James, who must have been listening on the net.

"Sir, we have Marines getting shot up and dying down there. If you send strike package Bravo to grid 4QFJ789347322, I'm sure they would appreciate it," pleaded Mark, hoping to help out his fellow Devil Dogs.

"Stay on mission and maintain radio silence until you have some vital information benefiting us, Double Tap out," growled the stern voice before the radio fell silent.

They scanned the area with their scopes, furious they couldn't assist.

Thirty seconds after calling in the request, artillery could be seen pounding the vicinity where the insurgents were holed up and firing mortars and machineguns at the Marine platoon.

From the mountain, Mark and Happy could see for miles. The M982 Excalibur 155-mm GPS guided munitions have a range of 36 kilometers, and with precise, thunderous explosions were destroying numerous mud-walled homes on the outskirts of what the Marines called the "Fish Tank" in the Brown Zone, southeast of Route 611.

Mark and Happy both knew why they were there, but neither could stand idly by and watch their fellow Americans and service-men get killed or wounded if they could do something about it.

"Score one for the good guys," cheered Happy as he initiated a high-five with Mark.

"It looks like the grid coordinates you gave me were spot on," Mark said.

"They always are, brother."

Once the bombardment stopped, the dust began blowing away, slowly making scorched earth and craters visible, even from so far away.

"I'm going to give the platoon commander down there a little advice, what's their frequency?" Mark said after watching for a few minutes.

"Don't do it, man. You remember what the colonel did last time?"

"I have to, or more good men are going to die for no reason."

"If the colonel gets word of what you did, make sure he's aware Happy had nothing to do with it," he said and reluctantly gave Mark the encrypted frequency the Marines were using.

"Why do you do that?"

"Do what?"

"Talk about yourself in the third person. It's just plain wrong, man," Mark said with a smirk.

Happy muttered softly and went back to watching the area through his spotting scope, waiting for something — *anything* — interesting to happen in their area of operation.

"Blackjack two-seven, this is Zeus, over," Mark said into the radio.

"Zeus... this is Blackjack two-seven. Go ahead with your traffic, over."

"I need to speak with Blackjack two-seven actual."

"Roger that, wait one."

"This is Blackjack two-seven," said a new voice over the radio moments later.

"Lieutenant," began Mark.

"Yes sir," said the Marine.

"Son, you had better get your head out of your ass and learn how to read a map instead of watching your Marines get cut down while you hide behind a rock. Do you understand me?"

Mark looked through his spotting scope, watching the Marine platoon.

"Who is this?" the lieutenant inquired, standing up and looking around.

"Your worst nightmare *and* your guardian angel. I *will* be watching you — Zeus, from Olympus, out."

Mark swapped frequencies back to the one they were supposed to be using. "I knew he'd be a lieutenant, damn butter bars," he said with a slanted smile while pulling on his goatee.

"We have movement," replied Happy with a grin. He repeated his comment over the net for command to hear, as well.

He and Mark were watching a convoy roll along a dirt road in the next valley over while trying to see through the dust and heat waves rising off the dry ground in the hot afternoon sun.

"Roger that, we see them, as well," command radioed. "You're clear to exfil once the trucks leave your line of site, as long as no stragglers can be seen. Proceed to Checkpoint Betty and move to landing zone Echo for extract. Your ride will be en route shortly, over."

"Lima Charlie, Deadeye out," ended Happy.

The men riding in old Russian trucks in the valley below stopped to check something in one of the vehicles. Another had its hood up and a column of steam rose from the engine. Each one of the rigs had covers over the beds to conceal what was inside. The trucks spent little time in the open, and heavy security surrounded them, most armed with AK-47s. They even had flank security pushed out about 50 meters off the road on either side with PKM belt-fed, light machineguns.

From what Mark and Happy could see from the ridge, most of the security detail were wearing traditional Afghan garb.

"How can they walk around in those dresses?" Happy asked Mark.

"They're called thawbs and kameezes buddy. It's what they wear."

"I know what they're called, but they still look like dresses to me. And I don't get the towel wrapped around their head, either. Never have."

"You mean the lunges?" Mark asked.

"No, the damn, turbans."

"They wear Turbans in other countries. You call these lungees in Afghanistan. It keeps 'em cool on hot days," Mark corrected. He knew he aggravated Happy and thought it amusing.

The men in the trucks didn't stay long and were rolling down the dirt road again, east toward Kandahar. More than likely heading to the Pakistan border from what they'd previously encountered.

The convoy was expected and was the reason Mark and Happy were there. Reliable intel on the ground gave them the location each time, and it hadn't been wrong so far.

After the trucks started moving, Happy called in the grid coordinates for the next General Atomics MQ-9 Reaper to move into the area of operation. With the range of the drone, it would be able to follow the trucks for some distance. The next team inserted several miles away could guide another in, if needed.

Mark looked at his Suunto X-Lander Wristop Navigator and noted the time in his water proof journal. The entire mission had been recorded on the drone's hard drive and real-time video transmitted back to command via satellite, but the good old-fashioned writing tablet brought attention to detail and situations others had missed on numerous occasions.

Mark and Happy sat up and secured their spotting scopes in their packs. The Barrett M107 .50-caliber rifle, being their primary long-distance weapon, broke down and fit nicely in a tan drag bag. They took turns watching the vicinity while the other took off their Gillie suit. Happy attached his tan FNH SCAR 17 chambered in 7.62x51 to his vest, as did Mark.

Mark put his Barrett cap on, and Happy a wide-brim camo Boonie cover. They started moving through the rough mountainous terrain to their designated pick-up point hours away.

Day-to-day operations changed as needed. Although their current mission of recon became uninteresting at times, it was relatively safe. They were getting paid extremely well for keeping tabs on enemy movement from a distance.

The mountains held pockets of locals and insurgents alike and had been encountered from time to time by them and other teams, and men had been lost. So far Mark and Happy had been lucky, but they knew it would be a matter of time before they found themselves in a fight for survival.

The men made their way to the LZ to await their helicopter ride back to Camp Leatherneck. The mountainous region made travel by foot difficult, especially with 130 pounds of gear and weapons, but this was what they lived for.

# Chapter Two
### Sangin River Valley, Northeast of the
### "Fish Tank"
### Monday, October 6th, 1059 Hours

"Men, this is why we're here — to win the hearts and minds of the locals. Now, keep 10 meters or more apart from the Marine next to you. If we're ambushed, I don't want to lose the whole platoon in the initial contact," boomed Lt. Brian Steel as the patrol walked on the sides of the dirt road out of the village, toward the mountains. Fresh out of Officer Candidate School, the second lieutenant and platoon commander showed his eagerness to do his duty for the Corps, God and country.

"Why does that honyak talk so much?" asked a large man carrying a Squad Automatic Weapon chambered in 5.56x45, spitting tobacco juice on the ground. He wiped his brow of the constant sweat excreting from his pores.

"Same fuckin' thing I was thinking," said the much smaller Marine to his left, wearing brown military-style spectacles, commonly referred to as birth control glasses due to how ugly they make anyone look. He appeared to be struggling with his gear and weapon in the early afternoon heat. "Aren't we supposed to be quiet and not draw attention to the patrol?"

"You men better be quiet back there," chimed the lieutenant in a loud voice. "I don't want the enemy to zero in on us because you wouldn't shut your sucks."

Without any warning, the Marine on point stopped, turned and slowly fell over, his M4 falling to the ground next to him. Dust flew up as he and his rifle hit the deck. A split second later the rest of the men heard the report from the rifle that fired the deadly round, probably from a sniper some distance away from the patrol.

"Incoming," yelled the lieutenant as he jumped to his left, ducking behind a large rock in front of him.

The Marines scrambled for cover, except the old gunnery sergeant walking with them. The scary-looking Marine didn't flinch as he grabbed the younger and less-experienced men one or two at a time and pointed them in the right direction while yelling for them to return fire. The gunny held a measure of respect among the men rivaled by few others.

An explosion detonated nearby and dust rose in a tiny mushroom cloud by some nearby bushes, then the screaming started.

"Wilson's been hit," someone yelled. Then, "Corpsman!"

A couple Marines hit trip-wires as they moved to cover which happened to be common for this district and more than likely, the reason for the attack. The enemy would start to shoot, forcing the coalition troops to head for cover and hit booby-traps the enemy set for them in miniature clusters of trees or bushes.

The popping sound of rifles firing grew in intensity like an old, stale pack of firecrackers lighting off on the Fourth of July. The gunny directed the machine-gun crews who began to lay down suppressing fire from different spots. The guns appeared to talk to one another as three to seven-round bursts could be heard one after the other. He told the mortar squad to lob in high-explosive rounds at the muzzle flashes in front of them. The thumping sounds of mortars could be heard, adding to the symphony of destruction with the rest of the weapons firing, far and near.

"Lieutenant!" barked Gunny Miller as he walked up to the large rock the officer and three other Marines had gathered behind. "Would you mind calling in some air support or artillery on those positions we're taking fire from? You men better get with the program and start shooting something!" he yelled to the other Marines shielded behind the rock.

"If I can find my map, Gunny, I will. Where's the map, Garza?" he said to the radio operator next to him.

"It's in your ruck-sack sir, top flap."

"Corpsman!" Gunny Miller yelled, while more rounds were twanging and hissing as they impacted nearby or ricocheted off the rock, throwing shrapnel and dust into the air.

A young man with Navy rank insignia on his collar and carrying a large, olive-drab green bag dove into position as more rounds could be heard zinging and snapping past Miller's head.

"Did you see the Marine get shot up there, doc?" Miller asked, pointing at a man on the ground.

"Yes, sir. I mean, *yes,* Gunny!"

"Then do your job and go get him before he bleeds out!"

"Garcia, can you cover me?" the Corpsman asked one of the Marines.

"No problem, Doc!" Garcia yelled over the gun-fire.

The Marine moved side by side with the Navy corpsman as they made their way up to the wounded Marine through a hail of bullets and clouds of dust. Gurgling sounds could be heard escaping his mouth as he choked on his blood from a sucking chest wound. The corpsman unhooked and pulled off the Marines gear. He applied large bandages to his front and back. The young man's brown eyes were huge, showing his fear. His pupils darted back and forth as he gasped for air. The men grabbed the wounded Marine and dragged him back to cover in a nearby irrigation ditch while bullets hit the ground, kicking up dust and ricocheting off rocks around them.

"Corpsman!" The yell was heard a few more times throughout the battle. After stabilizing the first Marine the Navy field doctor made his rounds under heavy enemy fire.

"Are you going to let them get away with shooting at us, Lieutenant?" demanded Miller.

"Gunny, I'm doing my best," stammered the young officer in a shaky voice while adjusting his helmet, which had slid way back on his head.

"Give me the map, son," Miller said, ripping it from the officer's hands.

Miller looked at it, then looked up at his surroundings and back at the map as the close popping sounds of M4 rifles and machineguns continued to fill his ears. He grabbed the handset from the radio operator and began to talk with authority. "Backlash, Backlash, this is Blackjack two-seven, over."

"Blackjack two-seven, this is Backlash, go ahead."

"Requesting fire mission Delta at the following coordinates..."

A high-pitched shriek could be heard over the sound of gunfire. Several more followed suit, then the first round fell to earth and detonated.

The area in front of the Marines lit up with explosions before Miller could finish calling in the artillery. He watched as high-explosive rounds pounded the vicinity from which they were taking hostile fire. The ground shook and the sound of thunder filled their ears. Even from half a kilometer away it temporarily masked most of the small-arms fire and yelling going on around them.

After a few short minutes the show ended as quickly as it had started.

"Backlash, Blackjack two-seven, I guess you boys already received the message. Blackjack two-seven out,"

Miller said into the radio before handing the handset back to the RO.

The Marines in the platoon stood up and started cheering. Secondary explosions were igniting as the cheering continued. Miller briefly pondered what had happened, then started issuing orders to the men.

Weapons from other Taliban militants in the area could be heard shooting off near them and the occasional bullet would hit nearby causing the Marines to shoot back in the direction of the incoming rounds. Murder holes, they were called — little holes the insurgents carved out of brick walls which allowed them to shoot and displace extremely fast. More times than not, the friendly forces never even saw a shooter. Countless troops felt like they were fighting ghosts.

A medevac had been called in for six wounded Marines, two of which were critical after losing limbs and large amounts of blood. The rest of the platoon carefully made their way down range to do an after-battle assessment of the enemy forces and weed out any stragglers. As the wounded waited patiently to be taken to safety, the loud *whup whup whup* sound of a helicopter could be heard, getting closer.

# Chapter Three
## Above Helmand Province, Afghanistan
### Monday, October 6th, 1448 Hours

"Did you guys see the arty show down in the Fish Tank earlier today?" the port-side door gunner asked on the com-link of the cigar-shaped Chinook. The dual-rotor aircraft, dating back to the early 1960s, looked to be as aerodynamic as a Greyhound bus with jet engines and wings.

Happy keyed his mic and beamed. "Hell yes. We had a bird's-eye view of that display of firepower."

Mark looked over at him with a smirk on his face.

Marines and others operating in the region called the sector the Fish Tank, because it's a hotspot for insurgent activity. The mud huts and restricting alleys reminded the friendly troops of what fish would swim through in a tank. Friendly forces named them murder holes, because far too frequently men were getting killed or severely wounded. That part of the Sangin River Valley has been called the Fallujah of Afghanistan.

The men continued to talk with the pilots and door gunners throughout the short, smooth flight through the mountains.

"Five minutes," barked the co-pilot.

Suddenly, bullets ripped through the fuselage of the dual rotor Marine transport, creating holes that let daylight shine through the thin aluminum skin of the aircraft. The starboard-side door gunner fell back onto the deck without making a sound. Bullets pierced the floor and walls. Hydraulic fluid from cut lines squirted everywhere like arterial spray, as if the aircraft itself bled, and the cabin filled with smoke from sparking electronics.

Without hesitation Mark stood up, took the cord attached to his headset off the wall and moved over to the empty door. He hooked into the intercom from the door gunner's panel with his headset, grabbed the M-134 General Electric mini-gun chambered in 7.62x51 and spooled it up.

"What do we have, boys?" he questioned the pilots while scanning the area.

"Starboard side," grunted the pilot, while fighting the controls.

The helicopter banked right to engage the threat and started taking small arms fire again. A rocket-propelled grenade fired at the aircraft. Mark saw the muzzle flashes and smoke trail from the grenade and lit the spot up with the mini-gun, firing on the targets below at a rate of 6,000 rounds per minute. The machine-gun growled like an angry beast as it threw hot lead to the earth like it had been sent back home, where it belonged.

The entire section of the ridge that held the threat sat in a cloud of dust a few minutes later when Mark ran out of ammo. The Gatling gun's barrels were red hot and smoking. He had only fired the weapon for a short time, but laid waste to the ground and everything on it.

While Mark leveled the ground below Happy took the Barrett M-107 out of its carrier, assembled it quickly and lowered the back ramp. He steadied the rifle in a cradle attached to the deck. A tail gunner would normally use this for hot landings and extractions. He flipped the scope covers open and started scanning below.

"Give me 15 degrees port," he told the pilot as he acquired targets and started to fire the powerful sniper rifle. *"Hit,"* he said on the intercom as he eliminated each target. He changed the large, 10 round magazine three times while taking out the threats. The Chinook flew in a slow orbit around the ridge to allow Mark and Happy to acquire and destroy the targets more easily.

Not long after it started, the engagement ended. The crew chief stabilized the door gunner who had been shot in the upper chest. The aircraft, despite the damage it had sustained, should make it back to base.

The pilot came across the intercom, "We've been ordered back to the ranch. A company from the Third

Battalion Fifth Marines will enter the area and do a battle damage assessment on the ridge."

Still fighting the controls, the pilot put the nose of the aircraft down by adding collective and moved over the desert toward safety at a fast pace after pouring on the throttle.

# Chapter Four
### Twenty Clicks Northeast of
### Patrol Base Bariolia
### Monday, October 6th, 1618 Hours

Upon entering the landing zone immediately south of their objective, the Marines were stunned by the devastation they saw after touching down in three Bell Boeing V-22B Ospreys. They contemplated the blood-stained ground and bodies strewn about as they exited the tilt-rotor aircrafts.

Capt. Dan Rogers paused for a moment. The cool mountain breeze mixed with the rotor-wash, felt refreshing when wearing so much gear. The smell of expended ordnance still lingered in the air even as the aircrafts dusted off.

"Give me flank security and overwatch in those rocks to the east," Rogers ordered over the radio to his platoon commanders. The Marines moved with purpose as the orders were received.

Rogers was a tall, muscular man from Indiana who had joined the Corps 10 years prior as an enlisted man after a short stint in college playing football. Before becoming an officer, he returned to college while on active duty and had gone to Officer Candidate School to further his career. Men like him are often referred to as Mustangs. The men with this title were revered by enlisted and commissioned alike and were more experienced than their peers in-grade. He managed a rapport with the enlisted on a level other officers envied.

Even though he shaved religiously, each morning he had a five o'clock shadow by noon. When on an exercise or mission he was able to grow a full beard in three days. He had always been the officer they sent into a village to talk with the tribal elders. It seemed they respected him even more when he sported his beard.

Once their surroundings were secured, the Marines fanned out and platoon commanders ordered their men to gather weapons and bodies. They also searched for intel. The assessment took hours and no enemy combatants were found alive. Flank security and overwatch checked in at regular intervals but had little to report.

The newer Marines were able to see firsthand what a 7.62x51mm mini-gun and a Barrett .50 BMG could do to flesh. Scores of the dead were missing limbs that had been ripped off by the cyclic rate of the Gatling gun and 690 grain bullets of the .50 cal.

Twenty-seven men and teenage boys had been killed. The troops piled up the enemy weapons and ammo outside the area of operation and set charges to blow them up. This would be considered a major victory for coalition forces in the fight to eradicate the enemy from the region.

After Rogers had called in the battle damage assessment, a small, black, MH-6 Little Bird helicopter flew around the perimeter as if surveying the scene. The aircraft finally landed nearby. A man in tan khaki pants and a short-sleeve polo shirt moved out of the helo and looked around. He walked over to the nearest Marine who brought the man to Capt. Rogers.

The man wore dark Oakley Batwolf sunglasses and carried a German H&K G-36 rifle in front of him with a Glock in a drop leg holster on his left leg. As he moved closer, the Marines could see his body armor, which held his extra magazines on the outside, in a slanted position.

"Capt. Rogers?" said the man as he pulled a toothpick out of his mouth and smoothed his thin black mustache.

"Yes sir. And you are?"

"I'm no one. I don't exist and was never here. But you can call me Smith."

"Yes, sir," said Rogers, pegging him for CIA.

"Hell of a job you and your men have done here. I'll need to see any Marines who took pictures with a camera or cell-phone."

"For what, sir?"

"Captain, I really don't like to repeat myself."

Rogers relayed the information to his radio operator and several Marines approached after he issued the request.

"Men, I need any cameras and phones you may have taken pictures with," Smith demanded.

After getting a nod from the captain, the Marines reluctantly handed over their property. The man looked through their devices, pushed buttons, then handed them back, except for one.

"Is this your wife, son?" he asked a private about a picture on his phone.

"She's my girlfriend, sir."

"Hot little lady. Hopefully, Jody doesn't stretch her out too much before you rotate back home," he chortled as he handed the phone back. "Marines, what you witnessed here is considered classified, and you cannot have pictures or talk about what you've seen. Am I clear?"

"Yes sir," they responded in unison.

"Captain, you and your men can leave now. Thank you for a job well done. Wait, could I see your notebook for a moment, please?"

Rogers reluctantly handed the notebook in which he'd been taking notes so he could accurately write his report back at base.

After looking it over the man ripped out a few pages.

"Captain, your report today will detail the uneventful patrol you and your Marines were on. Be as creative as you want to be," Smith said.

"Where did this patrol happen, Mr. Smith?"

"Pick a place you've been a dozen times," the man said. He walked away and lit the papers on fire with a gold Zippo, letting them blow away in the wind.

More black helicopters arrived alongside the troop transports sent to pick up the Marines.

Rogers knew protocol, and this had certainly not been it. Being a good Marine he wouldn't question, but he wouldn't forget.

# Chapter Five
### Camp Bastion Flight Line
### Monday, October 6th, 1512 Hours

The limping helicopter landed hard on the tarmac, jostling the men around the cabin and kicking up dust as they all did upon takeoff and landing. The black smoke spewing from the rear rotor was unusual, though, and the bird was met by crash and rescue vehicles just in case. A medical team, Col. James and a few men in sunglasses and khakis arrived as the bird shut down. Mark and Happy looked at each other before grabbing their gear and exiting the rear of the aircraft behind the wounded Marine and litter-bearers as the engines shut down.

"We need to debrief you two, *now*," commanded the colonel with a scowl on his face. Col. John James, a dumpy but muscular man with short graying hair, was a prior U.S. Army Special Forces officer. Everyone knew he had real-world experience and had seen his share of action, but the details were foggy. He didn't talk about what he had done or seen, a trait that was admirable and respected among the men, but sometimes his actions were questionable.

Mark and Happy glanced at each other with looks of bewilderment, but did as instructed.

They followed the officer, trailed by the other men.

They jumped into the waiting Humvees and drove through the base with almost no conversation, before stopping next to a few familiar buildings.

The men exited the vehicles, entered the operations center and walked toward the interrogation wing. After reaching their destination, Mark and Happy put their gear and weapons down at the rear of the room except for their sidearms, which remained holstered. They were asked to sit in chairs at the front table. The colonel stood off to the side.

A man set up a video camera and turned it on while a second man entered the room. He sported a loosely fitting black tie and short-sleeve white button-up shirt with sweat stains on the collar and under the arms.

"Son," he said with authority while looking at Happy. "What happened up there?"

"Well, sir," Happy began. "We were all just sittin' up there enjoying the flight back from our mission when we started receiving small arms fire from a ridge to our right. Mark here returned fire from the door gunner's window while I engaged from the rear to avoid being shot down, which is pretty much it, sir."

"Can you confirm this?" the man asked, looking at Mark.

"Yes, sir, I believe Happy summed up the events."

"Did either of you see this man in the mix below?" he asked, holding up a grainy photo.

"Can't say we did," Happy said, studying the picture. "It all happened pretty fast."

Mark shrugged his shoulders, looking from the picture to the man. "I saw lots of men with beards and they all died for Allah today. I couldn't tell from above, if one was taller than the rest."

"I want to thank you men for doing what you did to save the lives of the flight crew and weed out the insurgents."

"That's it?" Happy asked.

"Sir," Mark said as the man began walking away.

"What is it?" he replied, turning around.

"Why the CIA is involved in this matter? All we did was eliminate a tiny rebel force. It appears there's more to the story. What are you not telling us?"

The colonel shook his head ever so slightly to Mark's question.

"Son," he said. "You don't need to know anything else at this point—or ever. And from what I've heard about you, you had better tread lightly."

"Yes, sir," Mark said with a questioning look on his face.

Another man turned the camera off and took it and the tri-pod from the room. After they left, the colonel walked up to Mark and Happy. "What the hell were you thinking?"

"Something about this doesn't feel right and I was curious."

"He's right, Mitchell, you had better tread lightly," Col. James said. He left the room with a loud "Hmph."

Mark and Happy looked at each other, stood up and retrieved their gear.

"Beer?" Happy asked.

"Sounds good to me. Do you suppose we should shower first?"

"No way. We were only out for two days. I can't smell myself yet, so I'm sure we're good. Besides, Duke will let us know forthwith, if he wants us to leave."

Mark smiled in agreement and followed his companion outside.

On the way to the unofficial watering hole they stopped by their living quarters. The large concrete slabs surrounding the building opened up into a tented area with picnic tables and two grills made from a 55-gallon barrel someone had cut in half. A couple of men were sleeping in hammocks as Mark and Happy walked inside to drop their gear and secure their weapons in their rooms of what they and the other operators called "the Pit." Mark kept his Glock in its leg holster, as usual, but Happy always remained unarmed while on base. He believed if an incursion happened on post, there would be plenty of weapons to choose from within the first few minutes of an engagement. Mark agreed but felt that if he had a weapon to begin with, he would make it to another much faster. They complimented each other like that, making a great team.

After dropping their weapons and gear, they left the reinforced concrete-and-steel housing quarter to go relax. They noticed a commotion ahead near a row of Conex storage containers and went to investigate.

# Chapter Six
## Camp Leatherneck
### Monday, October 6th, 1627 Hours

Once they made it to the center of the crowd, they could see a Marine in a hand-to-hand conflict with a civilian contractor in tan khakis. Marines and sailors were cheering them on.

"Is that the best you have, boy?" taunted the contractor. With his shaved head and a short, graying beard, Mark guessed his age to be around 50.

"I'm going to fuck you up, old man," asserted the much younger, muscular Marine as he threw another elbow that connected with the man's face, immediately followed by a knee to his ribs.

The Marine looked to be winning. The contractor pulled a knife with a thin blade about 4 inches long and Mark stepped forward.

Mark moved in as the man started to slice the air where the Marine stood. The Marine started backing up toward the crowd, which also started moving away.

Mark blocked the advance and swept the man to the ground with a fast leg maneuver. The surprised man jumped back up and was about to attack when he realized who had intervened. He put his knife back in his boot, picked up his blue ball cap with an American flag embroidered on the front and moved away through the crowd.

Mark and Happy were civilian contractors working for the full-bird colonel, who ran the joint anti-terrorism taskforce to which they were attached, and answered to an agency that preferred not to be named. The command center worked independently from and in conjunction with the U.S. military machine. Assets were used whenever and wherever needed. Mark thought the man seemed familiar and was positive he had worked with him at one time or another. He obviously knew Mark, and more notably, his reputation.

The Marine thanked Mark and started to explain what happened but Mark put his hand up.

"I really don't care," he said. "We're all on the same side and you need to remember to save it for outside the fence, Devil Dog."

"Yes, sir," the Marine said, before walking away. A few other Marines joined him, patting him on the back to congratulate him on his victory.

The crowd had dispersed when Mark met up with Happy, who shook his head. "You're going to piss off the wrong person one of these days."

"The man would've gutted the Marine if I hadn't stepped in and you know it."

"I do, but there're plenty of other ways you could've handled it so he could save face."

"I agree, but diffusing the situation before it escalated even more felt like the most logical choice."

Happy walked through the crowd, Mark following behind him. They didn't always see eye to eye on everything, but they had each other's back.

The men entered the local pub, located in a sub-level of the Combined Aid Station.

Being early in the day there were only about a dozen people in the little room. By 1800 hours, the place would be packed beyond capacity. This is where the Marines, sailors and civilians attempted to relax and get some semblance of what they left behind back home. When they were hanging out, playing pool or darts and drinking beer, the war had been temporarily put in the rear-view mirror. The base commander knew about the not-so-legal establishment but overlooked it so his men and women could relax and hopefully be more effective when he needed them to be.

"What'll you two have?" asked Duke Thompson, the entrepreneur who brought the excitement to the place. In his late 40s now, he had been a Marine Corps major before retiring. His gray hair and scars showed a rough life, but he still had enough contacts on the base and in the country to build his establishment. He supplied several high-ranking officials with the comforts of home — whiskey, bourbon, cognac and even Cuban cigars for the men and women who allowed him to operate the business covertly. He even had a security team made up of off-duty Marines to make sure the unruly were handled. Guns and knives were checked at the door, and if you did something you weren't supposed to after drinking and leaving, you were subject to the uniform code of military justice. This rode a fine line, but each service member was responsible for their own decisions.

"Beer with a shot of tequila, and you can keep the training wheels," Mark said as Duke reached for a salt-shaker.

"Just a beer for me," Happy said.

They sat at the bar as more people started to show up. The shelves behind the counter were fully stocked with the same alcohol found in a bar back in the States, though no beer was on tap because it proved easier for Duke to discreetly bring in bottles and cans with normal supplies, than kegs. Pictures and posters of singers, rock stars and movie stars cluttered the walls. Dollar bills with cities, states and people's names written on them hung from the ceiling. Mark inhaled the smells of home as they walked through the smoke-filled cantina.

Laughter drew Mark's attention to the door. Sandy, the voice he had been so accustomed to hearing on the radio while on missions, walked in with a few other women. She saw him sitting at the bar and made her way to him, greeting other people along the way. A DOD contractor like him now, she had been an Army intelligence officer who worked at the Pentagon.

"Fancy meeting you here," she said as she finally made it to him, a smile brightening her face. "You did a good thing today for those Marines." She noticed Happy and put on a larger smile making her dimples stand out even more. "Both of you did."

Grabbing his beer, Happy stood up. "Thanks. I'll leave you two alone."

"No, you don't have to..." she started to say in her sweet Southern accent.

"It's all right," Mark said. "He isn't a very good conversationalist."

"I feel bad now. I didn't mean to run him off."

"It's OK. So tell me, what made the colonel change his mind and send artillery to the coordinates I called in?"

"The base commander, Gen. Moore, happened to be there when you called in and made the decision for him. After the coordinates you gave us were verified, we watched the whole thing on the big screen once the camera on the drone was pointed in the right direction."

"That's great news."

"The general did ask who you were and commended your actions to the room."

Mark's smile grew larger. "So, I won't be fired anytime soon?"

"It doesn't look like it."

Duke came over and set Sandy's usual on a white napkin — a Lemon Drop with a tiny pink umbrella in the glass. "Ron Moore is a hell of a Marine Corps officer," Duke said.

Sandy smiled at Duke, moved the glass and pulled a pen from her pocket. She appeared to write something on the napkin, thanked Duke and gave him a $10 bill. She leaned over to Mark. "I would love to keep talking to you, but, you *smell* terrible." She giggled and walked away.

"You do stink," Duke agreed.

"Thanks, buddy," Mark replied as he looked down at the napkin. It had a smiley face on it. Mark smiled, folded it and put it in his pocket. "I have to wonder why she was the only one who had the balls to tell me."

Duke laughed as Sandy looked back over her shoulder, smiling at the men. This prompted Mark to order one more shot, down his beer and head back to the barracks for a shower.

He stopped by the pool game Happy had weaseled himself into and informed him of his destination. Even on base, it was a good idea to have someone with you, or to let them know where you're going.

Outside, the sun had almost set and Mark paused to take in the distant mountains and fading red, yellow and blue colors of the horizon before entering "the Pit."

The building showed little signs of life, so he essentially had the run of the place. Mark turned on a community stereo with surround sound and AC/DC's "You Shook Me All Night Long" started pulsing from the speakers as he grabbed fresh clothes, a towel and shower gear from his locker.

The water flowed barely lukewarm, as usual, but felt good nevertheless. He lathered up slowly, savoring the refreshing smell, sound and feel of clean. He let the water pour over him, enjoying yet another comfort that reminded him of home.

He and Happy would be gone for days, sometimes weeks on missions, so he always looked forward to a shower upon returning.

As the water turned cold, Mark turned off the faucet. He heard footsteps echoing through the empty barracks and wondered if Sandy had decided it was time to take the next step past flirtation. He had nearly finished drying off when a grenade rolled into the stall.

"Son of a bitch," he exclaimed as his reflexes and training took over.

# Chapter Seven
## "The Pit"
### Monday, October 6<sup>th</sup>, 1742 Hours

The thought of being fragged in the shower while naked wasn't on his list of ways to die, but he suddenly realized the possibility.

Mark dove for cover around the corner of the brick stall as the grenade detonated in a thunderous explosion, throwing shrapnel throughout the room. Water sprayed from broken pipes and concrete dust filled the building as the base alarm sounded. Quick reaction squads moved in to secure the area.

Stunned but unhurt, he found his now-soaked towel on the floor and moved out of the room to get dressed and assess what had happened.

As Marines in full combat gear cleared the vicinity and entered the structure, Happy found Mark sitting on a bench in the locker room with his wet towel still wrapped around him.

"What the hell happened?" he asked Mark.

"It looks like I made another enemy."

"Are you hurt? I can take you to the aid station."

"Not a scratch, but it's a little hard to hear," he yelled, half sarcastically, "I'll be fine."

"This has been one hell of a day, brother."

"You can say that again."

Happy noticed Mark held something in his hand.

"Whatcha have there?"

"It's nothing," Mark replied, putting the picture back into his locker.

"Is that Michael's photo?"

"Yeah. It must have fallen out while I grabbed my clothes."

"I'm here for ya if you ever want to talk," Happy said.

"I know. Thanks."

The dust still settled in the building as Mark put his clothes on.

"It looks like a single fragmentation grenade detonated in the shower room," said a familiar voice, prompting Mark and Happy to look behind them. The Marine grinned and leaned against the lockers, while his partner, a long haired German shepherd, sat patiently by his side. She was one of numerous canines in the country working with Marines to help locate IEDs, off leash.

"I could've saved you some time, it rolled right by me," Mark said as he stood up from the bench by his locker. "They'll let anyone in here, won't they?"

Staff Sgt. Dan Brody was an explosive ordnance disposal technician and an old friend of Mark's. He had grown up in the same small town on the Oregon coast.

They spent as much time together as they could when they were in the same theatres of operation.

"It's good to see you, brother," Dan said as they shook hands and hugged. "Who the hell did you piss off this time?"

"I have an idea, but won't know for sure until I see his face."

"You want to go see him now?" Happy asked, wondering who Mark thought it had been.

"Now is as good a time as any. Dan, I'd love to catch up with you, but I need to get to the bottom of this."

"I understand. If you guys need any help, let me know."

"The offer is appreciated, but this shouldn't take long to figure out," Mark said as he petted Schnell. Happy reached out to pet her as well, but she growled at him in a low, "don't mess with me" tone.

Dan and Mark laughed as Happy quickly moved his hand out of the way. Schnell wagged her tail.

"I've warned you before. She only likes certain people," Dan said.

Mark dressed and grabbed something out of his locker before he and Happy left the building in search of the contractor Mark had encountered earlier. The man was the only one who came to mind who might have the balls to attempt something like fragging another team member. Mark couldn't remember anyone else he had offended lately, at least not to the degree of attempted murder.

# Chapter Eight
## Under Camp Leatherneck
### Monday, October 6th, 1824 Hours

Scores of people knew about the tunnels under the base, but most hadn't ever been in the section that was controlled by active-duty Special Forces personnel and civilian contractors. It was a city unto its own.

According to locals, the underground passages had existed for hundreds, if not thousands of years. They were the main reason for locating the Marine base there, along with the conjoined Camp Bastion, the main British military base in the country, which already had an airfield. Sections of the tunnels had been expanded and bomb shelters were built by the U.S. Navy Seabees — in case of an attack.

After walking down three flights of dimly lit stairs, Mark and Happy moved into the main shaft under the troop barracks.

"When was the last time you were down here?" Happy asked as he looked at the water crystals on the walls reflecting off the dull lights hanging from the ceiling.

"It's been a few months and it always look different. Like these tunnels and rooms."

They passed by multiple spurs. Some kept going, but others looked as if construction had recently started. They noticed multiple locked doors along the way.

"I wonder if this damp smell will ever get better?" Happy considered as the pungent air filled his nostrils.

"From what I've been told, they only control the humidity in certain places, mainly the living quarters."

The winding channels of reinforced earth and concrete led them to the lair they had come to visit. A couple of men, acting as doormen, were sitting at a little table playing cards outside the entrance to a large room. They looked up as Mark and Happy came into view.

With a casual nod in their direction, Mark confidently walked through the door and into another hall. Happy walked close behind and also said nothing. If you looked like you belonged, people usually assumed you did.

The poorly lit hallway opened up into a bright room with men milling about inside. The cathedral ceiling disappeared into a dark void in some places the light didn't reach. Plywood structures lined the walls. Office space and rooms were built for specific purposes. It was the staging area and living quarters for much of the base's behind-the-scenes operations. Men from some of the military branches and a couple of contracting companies called this place home. They referred to this section as "The Dungeon."

"Something I can help you boys with?" asked a man who stood slightly taller than Mark or Happy and had at least 40 pounds of pure muscle on each of them. He wore no shirt, exposing tattoos covering his chest, stomach and both arms. This man looked like he meant business and didn't back down.

"I need to talk to Memphis," Mark said.

"Do you and crater face have an appointment?"

"We don't need one," Happy replied, losing his smile.

"You do if I say you do," the large man retorted.

"Snake, I can smell your testosterone from here. Who wants to see me?" called a voice from a side room.

"It's Mark Mitchell."

"Well, why didn't you just say so? Come on in."

Mark stared a hole through the tattooed man as he walked by. Happy backed up to a wall and waited in the shadows nearby.

Walking into the room, Mark did a visual recon. He noticed several wooden crates along the walls, stacked three deep and five high.

"What can I help you with this evening, Mitchell?"

Memphis was a tall, thin, muscular man with shoulder-length black hair and a short matching beard. Rumor had it he had once been a member of SEAL Team 4, but no one beside him and the men he served with knew for sure. He currently ran in-country operations for a company named Executive Security. As far as most people knew, it was a multi-national organization made up of a few millionaires and billionaires who owned and operated it. Memphis commanded mercenaries from too many countries to name to perform operations off the books, which no one else had the stomach to do.

"I need to find a man and kill him," Mark said, handing Memphis a cigar, which he eagerly took.

"And — who might this man be?" Memphis ran the length of the Havana under his nose. "Cuban. You sure know how to charm, Mitchell."

"He would be the man who tried to frag me in the shower about an hour ago, and obviously failed. Listen, Memphis, I know this guy works for you and you may or may not give him up. But you have to agree, what he did was pretty fucked up."

"From what I heard, you made him look weak in front of the whole base. Some argue you deserved it and whatever else you have coming," he replied while cutting the end off the cigar and lighting it with a match, then slowly rotating it and inhaling the sweet aroma.

"Have coming? He would've killed the Marine, a fellow American, if I hadn't intervened."

"Is this true, Nate?" Memphis asked. A man walked out of the shadows behind the desk as Memphis exhaled more smoke rings.

Mark instantly pulled his sidearm and pointed it at the man from the fight earlier.

"I wouldn't do it, Mark," Memphis began. "He's my problem and I will deal with him accordingly. He will, however, be leaving you alone as long as you and your friend leave right now. What are your thoughts, Jackal?"

Another operator with a long black beard and bulging biceps escorted Happy into the room at gunpoint.

"Sorry to bother you, Memphis," Mark said, holstering his Glock and showing his empty hands. "You gentlemen have a nice night."

"We still have an opening for you here, Mark, whenever you're ready to make some real money," Memphis offered.

"I'm doing just fine in my current job, thanks," Mark told him.

He and Happy walked out of the room and continued down the hallways until they were alone.

"Did you accomplish your mission?" asked Happy, half sarcastically.

"I believe Memphis. He's a bastard and a thug, but he's a stand up guy otherwise. If he says it, then it will happen."

"Did he offer you a job back there?"

"Every time I see him he does. I've turned him down each time."

"Who do they work for?"

"A company called Executive Security. Basically, Mercenaries-R-Us."

The rest of their walk up to the surface was quiet. After they reached the top of the stairs, Happy finally spoke up. "I forgot to tell you, Col. James has a new mission for us. The briefing is at 0300 tomorrow."

"Any idea what it is?"

"Nope. He wouldn't even give me a hint."

"All right brother, we better get some chow and rest if we're going on back-to-back missions."

Mark and Happy walked over to the mess hall to eat dinner and get some much-needed rest before the next mission. Mark was quiet during the meal of meat-loaf, green beans and biscuits. His mind worked over-time as he picked at his food.

"Do you really want me to simply forget about what he did?" Nate questioned.

"I've known Mark Mitchell for years and he oper-ates by the book," Memphis replied. "He won't be a problem as long as you leave him alone."

"What about the mission? Should we worry about him interfering?"

"No, but if it comes to it, he'll need to be taken out."

Nate left the room with a sadistic smile on his face, mumbling under his breath.

"Snake, get in here!" Memphis demanded.

"Yes, boss," answered the large man with a deep voice.

"Contact our man in the field and let him know the next shipment will be dropped off at this location instead," Memphis said, handing Snake a piece of paper with grid coordinates on it.

"Will do, boss. Are we still providing security for the decoy, too, or should we let them handle it?"

"Tell our contact the locals will need to go this one alone. We've more imperative undertakings."

"Roger that," Snake said and left the room.

Memphis turned around and looked at the stack of crates. He already knew what was inside, but wanted another look. He opened a box with his Bowie knife and stared at the contents. The glare from the reflection of the overhead lights was nearly too much to take in, causing him to squint. A tentative smile started across his face and quickly disappeared as he closed the lid, hammering it back down with the butt of the knife's handle.

# Chapter Nine
### Mission Brief, Code Name:
### "Overshadow"
### Tuesday, October 7th, 0303 Hours

"Gentlemen, good morning," boomed the colonel, as everyone stretched and yawned while taking their seats at the long wooden table in the briefing room.

Bravo and the other teams who made up the task-force were mainly American, although there were a few British, Canadian and German members, as well. Each team was well suited for a specific role for each mission. Each member had been prior military of some kind and reported to the colonel above anyone else, even their own governments. The tension between the teams was sometimes explosive, but when it came down to it in the heat of battle, brotherhood, camaraderie and consummate professionalism had always prevailed.

"First, I want to start off by saying the attempt on Mitchell's life is still under investigation. We're considering every possible reason for the attack and are confident we will find the perpetrator or perpetrators quickly. The men's showers will be closed until the forensics team is done collecting evidence. Reconstruction will begin as soon as possible. In the mean time, the women's showers next door have a posted rotation time for you to follow. Does anyone have any questions?"

Nobody said anything. But, with raised eyebrows and shaking heads, you could see the wheels turning in their minds. Each understood the reason for the attempted fragging, whether it had been warranted or not.

Col. James moved on. "A few of us put this operation together last night in secrecy. We believe there may be a leak within this organization. We still don't know for sure whether it's a person on the taskforce, or radio transmissions being compromised. This is a live operation and all standard mission parameters will be followed. We will try to flush out the traitor or traitors as the mission moves forward. Each team will get their assignments from me separately, and in private. We will then try and determine where the breach is."

Happy spoke up. "Colonel, what kind of leak are we talking about? Is it information regarding missions, or personnel?"

"That's still classified."

"Sir, if I may," began Valentine, a former Delta Force operator with short blonde hair and a dark tan.

"Yes, Val, what is it?"

"If there is a leak, and he's in this room, don't you imagine he would simply not do anything to compromise himself since you suspect him already?"

"You have a valid point, and it has already been factored in."

Valentine shook his head. Everyone knew he was right, but figured there must have been a reason for the way the colonel played his cards.

"Six, two-man teams will be inserted in this valley," started Sandy, with the familiar soft twang, as she turned on the Power Point, displayed across the large screen at the front of the room. A map of the target area popped up and she used a laser pointer to show the location of insertion.

"Your separate missions will be explained to you discreetly for security reasons, as the colonel stated. We will be keeping tabs on a convoy of vehicles believed to be smuggling Taliban extremists, drugs and possibly weapons out of the country and into Peshawar, Pakistan and possibly other places, too. Evidence suggests this convoy, and the others you've been providing intel on, have something to do with this training camp in the Hindu Kush Mountains."

Another picture displayed on the screen. This one was a satellite image of a training area with an obstacle course, tires and numerous vehicles partly hidden by camo netting. More pictures were shown of fighters in large groups loading wooden crates onto trucks.

The screen turned black and a picture of a man with a long black and gray beard popped up. Sandy began again. "This is a man who we believe to be a lieutenant for..."

"I'm sorry, can you go back to the last picture before this man?" interrupted Mark.

Sandy clicked back to the image of the crates on the ground. Several of the operators gave Mark a questioning look.

"Do we know what's in the wooden crates?" Mark asked.

"We can only speculate about drugs or weapons being inside. We have a reliable contact inside the camp, but the contents are still unknown to him and are guarded closely by only a few men who are completely loyal to the cause."

"How reliable is this guy?" Val asked in a condescending tone. "Could he be the leak?"

"And this is what they're smuggling across the border?" Mark broke back in.

"Among other items, yes."

"Thanks, Sandy, please continue."

Valentine sat in his seat shaking his head about being ignored.

Sandy paused and gave Mark a strange look, then looked cautiously at the colonel before continuing with the rest of the briefing.

Once she finished, the colonel took over again.

"Echo Team, stay. The rest of you go to the Pit and gear up. Ms. Ackerman has a list of gear you will need for this op. Each team will be inserted at different times and locations. If you have any further questions, you can ask me while I brief you. You're dismissed gentlemen."

Echo Team consisted of the two Canadians on the taskforce. They weren't well liked by the other members because they caused unnecessary waves, calling it, "following protocol."

"What was with the line of questioning back there?" Happy asked Mark as they walked into the locker room.

"You'll find out soon enough, brother," he replied in a low voice so no one else could hear them.

They put on their gear, proceeded to the ammo dump to gather more ammo and other pertinent ordnance the operation required and waited their turn to get their private mission briefing.

They watched the other teams enter the room and leave not long after.

"Bravo Team, you're up." Mark and Happy walked into the designated room.

"Men, you and the other team members were chosen for this taskforce because of your outstanding records of service in your particular fields of expertise, but no one is beyond reproach until my internal investigation can clear you. I want to believe neither of you could be involved, or any of the other teams, for that matter," the colonel said.

"Involved in what, sir?" Happy asked.

"As I explained, I can't say until we figure out exactly where the problem lies."

"Sir, are those crates only being shipped out of country, or are they being brought in, as well?" Mark asked.

"Why would you ask me that?" The colonel looked surprised.

"Just being thorough, sir."

"Mitchell, if you have information that can help or hinder my investigation, you'd better tell me."

"I've seen crates similar to the ones in the picture, but I'm not sure it means anything."

"Where did you see them?"

"At the supply building," Mark told him.

Happy gave him a "what the fuck" look, but quickly controlled it in front of the colonel.

"I'll have someone go check it out," the colonel said, before pointing at the map in front of them. "Now, on to your mission. You'll be inserted southeast of the Panjshir Valley behind this mountain, by a Super Stallion. This is landing zone, Phoenix. You will then move northwest to waypoint Scottsdale, here, and on to your objective, Tucson, here. You will check in on the encrypted net every two hours after your initial contact upon landing, as well as from the waypoint and your objective. Your call sign for this mission is Apache. Command is Cherokee."

Happy pulled out a pencil and notepad and began writing everything down.

"You have two mission priorities. You will be keeping an eye on Delta Team, here," he continued, pointing out their location on the map. "The second is the road in the valley where the convoy will pass you, here. You will provide sniper cover for an assault team we inserted last night. They will detonate charges in the road disabling the lead and rear trucks. They will then move to intercept while you and Delta cover them from the ridges, here and here. An AC-130 Spectre gunship from Bagram Airbase will be on station for tasking if you believe they're needed, but check with me first, before using them. A quick-reaction force from Special Operations Command will be on standby here, if they're needed, as well. They and two Super Cobra attack helos will be inbound and on station within 30 minutes of getting the call."

"Where will the other teams be?" Happy asked.

"They have their own mission parameters and will execute them. Don't worry about the other teams."

"Are there any civilians or combatants in the AO we should be aware of?" Mark asked.

"Satellite imagery is fresh and the surrounding area has been monitored for the last three days by drones. There should be nothing else moving down there, but we will relay any new info as it comes in. Do you have any other questions?"

"No, sir," they said in unison.

"Good. Then go out to the flight line and board your designated bird for insertion."

# Chapter Ten
### The Ridge, LZ Phoenix
### Tuesday, October 7th, 0343 Hours

The other teams were already on board when Mark and Happy walked up the ramp. They were sitting some distance from each other and the windows had been blacked out. After they were on board, the General Electric T64 power plants of the Sikorsky aircraft started up and the ramp closed, drowning out some of the noise.

Each of the teams had been on missions requiring multiple insertions at alternate LZs before, but this one had most of them on edge.

"This is just weird," Happy said to Mark as they sat down.

"I agree, brother, but it's for good reason. This isn't the first investigation we've been through, and it won't be the last."

The aircraft lifted off the tarmac and rapidly gained altitude. Mark looked at his watch and took a mental note of the time. They couldn't see where they were, but their ears popped several times as they flew toward their destinations.

After 40 minutes of flight time, the crew chief walked over to them and yelled, "Ten minutes!" over the sound of the mechanics.

Mark gave him a thumbs up and smacked Happy on the shoulder, waking him. They checked their gear, com-links and weapons one last time and lowered their goggles from the top of their helmets. The ramp opened and darkness filled the space in front of them.

The crew chief walked to the ramp with a thick rope, attached it to a swivel bar and motioned for them to get up. Mark and Happy moved toward the open door and ramp to prepare to fast-rope to the ground while the helicopter hovered.

A green light appeared near the opening, indicating it was time to go. The crew chief couldn't be heard over the loud noise of the massive rotor, but his lips read, *"Go, go, go!"*

Happy slid down the rope first, followed immediately by Mark after he tightened the Velcro straps on the thick leather gloves he used for fast-roping.

Once on the ground, they both maneuvered behind some rocks for cover from the rotor-wash as the helo moved away from the LZ throwing anything lighter than a rock or a tree about the area. After the large bird moved out of sight and they could hear again, the chirping of crickets and creaking of trees filled their ears, as a slight breeze blew on the mountain top.

They paused to take off their helmets and goggles and swapped them for their favorite soft-covers, then Happy grabbed the radio. "Cherokee, this is Apache, radio check, over."

"Apache, this is Cherokee, Lima-Charlie, over."

"Cherokee, we are at Phoenix, en-route to Scottsdale, over."

"Roger that, Apache. Heading to Scottsdale."

"Apache, out," Happy said.

Mark consulted his GPS and he and Happy moved through the rough terrain of shale rocks and thick brush with the aid of a tiny amount of moonlight still shining. Almost an hour later the first weak rays of light could be seen in the distance.

The target convoy coming out of the Hindu Kush Mountains wasn't expected until late the following morning. The main assault force was already in place and the sniper teams were being inserted above the Panjshir Valley. It would take each team some time to reach their objectives from their initial landing zones. Stealth was a priority. If one of the locals or nomadic tribes saw a team member, the whole mission could be blown.

The sun blossomed on the horizon in the cloudless sky. Bright rays of light brought the valley to life. The morning dew absorbed into their clothing as they pushed up the side of the peak, but would dry as the temperature rose.

Bravo Team made great time despite the weight they carried through the rough terrain. The gear, weapons and ammo were essential to their mission. Mark and Happy were both in top physical shape, owing to a disciplined exercise regimen they followed on base. Their lives and those of their team members depended on it.

Mark stopped to take a break, survey the area and check their gear. They needed to make it to the waypoint before dark and dig in until morning before continuing to their objective.

Happy dropped his pack on the ground, took off his camouflaged Boonie cover and wiped sweat from his brow. "I'm sure going to miss this place when I head to my next assignment, brother."

Mark looked back at him and swallowed a large swig of water from his canteen. "You going somewhere I don't know about, sweetheart?"

"Not anytime soon, but when I do, I sure hope it's tropical."

Mark smiled at the sarcasm in Happy's voice. "You're not getting too old for this shit, are you?"

"Hell no. I can still run circles around you, boy!"

"I'd like to see you prove it, but we have a mission to accomplish and I, for one, always accomplish mine."

Happy gave him a thumbs-up.

A miniature gray and tan lizard, one of numerous species found in the country, looked at them from the top of a large rock. It had smooth scales, a blue metallic portion under its mouth and a purple patch behind its front legs.

Mark and Happy surveyed the area before being satisfied they could move on. They stowed their gear and continued to climb the mountain. Once they reached the ridge they could relax a little. The waypoint lurked beyond it, about six kilometers away from their current position. They were confident they would reach it by nightfall and move to their objective early the next morning, as long as nothing unforeseen happened.

Not long after reaching the ridge, as the late afternoon shadows grew increasingly longer, Mark looked at his GPS. "Two more clicks, and we can look for a place to spend the night."

Happy, out of breath, nodded.

They moved out, this time downhill. The loose shale gave way under their Lowa Renegade boots. But even with their heavy gear, the boots made walking on the rough terrain much easier.

Twenty minutes later, Mark held up a fist, making Happy freeze in place. After a few seconds of hearing nothing, he quietly asked Mark, "What is it?"

"I thought I heard voices, but it must've been the wind or birds."

They stood still and listened, but heard only their hearts thumping. They made their way down to the main tree line of a lower ridge, spotting a group of pine trees surrounded by rocks that would provide adequate cover for the night. Their former Marine reconnaissance training prepared them for the mission at hand.

Happy took his pack off and began moving brush from the inside to the outside of the area while Mark covered him from above. He made a hide, large enough for the two of them.

"Son of a bitch," Happy gasped, as he bolted out of the cluster of trees.

"What is it?" Mark whispered on their com-link.

"A damn viper, that's what."

Mark let out a quiet laugh while making his way down to him. He took off his pack, unhooked his rifle from his vest and moved inside with a flashlight. He came right back out with a three-foot serpent wrapped around his arm. It hissed as Mark held it tightly behind its head.

"Get the fucking snake away from me," warned Happy quietly, but with an even tone.

"It only wanted to cuddle with you, man."

Mark quietly laughed at his friend. He knew how much snakes scared Happy. Spiders and scorpions weren't his favorites, either, even though he would catch them and enter them in fights on base. This never made much sense to Mark, because this hard charger had no qualms with slitting a man's throat and bleeding him dry. He would even smile while doing it, depending on his mood.

Mark put the reptile in a little leather pouch he pulled out of a pocket on his vest. "We can eat her later."

"You can eat the damn thing if you want, but I want nothing to do with it!"

"Are you about done?"

"I was until it showed up. We can move in now, unless there are more of them."

"I don't believe so," Mark said with a smile. "Call Command and give them a sit rep."

"Roger that."

After the check-in, Happy settled down and ate an energy bar while Mark stood overwatch 50 meters above the hide. As the sun moved closer to the horizon, it spilled red, orange and purple through the valley below. Mark moved back to join Happy.

Three hours after they made it to waypoint Scottsdale and moved into their hide for the night, they heard movement below and to their left flank. Twigs snapped and rocks were moved from their resting places. Some tumbled downhill and bounced off others. In the still of the night, the noises echoed through the trees. Mark and Happy attached their night vision monoculars to their helmets and put them on. They looked at one another and gave hand signals after they were activated. Each of them produced Beretta M9 9mm handguns from holsters and screwed on suppressors.

Whispers were heard through the brush concealing their position. They saw tiny lights covered with cloth to limit the distance of the beams.

In their hide, Mark and Happy couldn't be seen, but could be discovered if the people entering the area and started poking around. Happy turned the radio off so it wouldn't give away their position if Command called them.

Before long, they could see four men about 10 meters in front of them, carrying two large cases. The men were speaking in Dari, the most common language in the country. Two of them transitioned to Arabic a few times and made references to Syria and Iran. Mark's instinct indicated they were more than likely bad guys. Without the ability to send radio traffic about the combatants, they would need to make a decision on their own as to how to proceed.

The four men opened the cases and set up rifles behind a cluster of rocks. Mark and Happy knew what they had to do.

In the distance, screeches, growls and barks of the rhesus macaque could be heard piercing the silence of the calm night. The monkeys are native to Afghanistan and various other countries in Central, South and Southeast Asia. U.S. military troops and civilian contractors avoid the animals whenever possible. Severe bites from monkey attacks happened more regularly than one would imagine.

Happy took the first watch, while Mark tried to sleep as crickets chirped in the entire area. Three out of the four insurgents slept while one kept watch. Two of the enemy combatants snored loudly and were constantly woken up by the man on watch and told to be quiet.

It would be a long night for Mark and Happy, but it was merely in a day's work for them.

"Sir, Bravo Team has missed three scheduled check-ins, since reaching their way-point at 1745 last night," said a Marine corporal from the communications center, sporting a high-and-tight haircut showing his receding hairline.

The young lieutenant on duty in the command center stood motionless for a few seconds.

"Should we wake the colonel?" asked the corporal.

"Who's on Bravo Team?"

"Mark and Happy, sir."

"How were their coms when they last checked in?"

"Crystal, sir."

"I'm sure there's a very good reason for not checking in or answering our calls. Besides, we're not sending the QRF or anyone else out, at least until daylight as per the SOP for this op. Keep trying to contact them and keep me apprised. I'll see if we can push an AWACS in for a fly-over."

"Roger that, sir."

The skeleton crew on night shift continued to monitor the teams in the field. With the exception of two teams failing to check in, the mission moved along as planned. The lack of communication could be for a number of reasons.

The mountainous regions of the country were well known for having spotty radio communication and dead spots. Protocols and contingency measures were in place to make sure each operation happened without a hitch, but there were times when troops were in contact and no one knew until it was too late. The men in the communications center hoped this was not one of those times.

# Chapter Eleven
## The Ridge, Waypoint Scottsdale
### Wednesday, October 8th, 0512 Hours

Early the next morning, the four combatants woke up and one started a tiny fire in front of the hide, with the sides covered by slabs of rock to hide the flame. The youngest, began cooking rice for them to eat with a batch of roht, an Afghan round, sweet flatbread, after he made a pot of kahwah tea. The scent of the spices used in the green, or chai tea still lingered in the morning air even as the food was prepared. The smell made Mark hungry.

Mark woke Happy as dawn was breaking, enhancing the scene in front of them. It remained dark inside their lair so they still had their night vision activated. Mark tapped Happy on the chest and gave him the signal to kill the two men on the right and he would wound the two on the left. Once they started shooting, they would need to move quickly to silence the wounded men.

With daylight creeping over the mountains, the wind started to blow ever so slightly. The creaking of the surrounding trees would aid Bravo Team in what they were about to do.

As the four sat around the fire eating bread and drinking tea out of petite glasses, called istakhans, Mark and Happy prepared to attack.

Before the two men on the left could register the soft whispers of the handgun's suppressors, their two companions fell to the ground dead. The men on the left felt a sting in their legs while trying to figure out what was happening. They didn't see or hear anything else until the ground under the trees behind them came alive, and what looked like two demons, charged out of it and ran straight toward them.

Mark and Happy were on the two wounded men within seconds. The insurgents were either too confused or too scared to make any sounds. Either way, it worked in Bravo Team's favor.

Once flex-cuffs and gags were put on the enemy combatants, Happy grabbed the handset of the radio, turned it on and checked in with Command.

"Cherokee, this is Apache, over."

He had to repeat his call three times before he received a response.

"Apache, this is Cherokee, we read you Lima, Charlie. You boys OK out there?"

"Roger that, Cherokee. We had a sleep-over last night and just had an early morning pillow fight. The party has broken up and we're now having tea. How copy, over."

"Literally having tea," Mark said as he poured a cup for himself. Happy shook his head.

There was a moment of silence before the radio came back to life.

"Uh... Roger that, Apache... How many left, over?"

"Two out of four and the conversation just started. Will relay info on the move to Tucson, momentarily. Apache out."

Happy rejoined Mark, who had already begun questioning the prisoners.

"Were you able to get anything out of them?" Happy asked.

"They say they're only goat herders."

"Well, I suppose we're going to have to get creative."

Happy pulled down the pants of the younger of the two combatants. Pulling out his Marine KA-BAR knife with a 7-inch blade, Happy, sliced the blade through a large tree branch to show how sharp it was. The man understood his intentions and started singing like a canary on a calm summer morning as he attempted to pull his pants back up.

The other man pleaded with the younger man, "Don't tell them anything!"

Mark smacked him on the head and warned him, putting his gag back in place. "Shut your mouth or I'll let my friend use his knife on you."

The man stayed temporarily silent until more vital information flowed from the younger man's mouth.

Mark's warnings to the older man fell silent, prompting Happy to walk him a few meters out of view and end his life.

Once the young man had finished talking, Mark dispatched him quickly from behind.

"What did he say?" Happy asked when he came back, dragging the other insurgent's corpse. He used the leftover tea to put out the fire.

"They were hired to kill Americans — the two of us, specifically. They were told we would be here. They were given the rifles and the coordinates to our location. This is getting serious."

"You're right, brother. We better get going."

Happy called Command on the radio to advise them of their situation while Mark pulled the bolts from the two Istiglal semi-auto sniper rifles chambered in 14.5x114 mm. The rifles were designed and manufactured in Azerbaijan for anti-material purposes, but they were used on people, too. The enemy combatants were going to use them on American and coalition forces, which is against the Geneva Convention. The laws were designed to limit the barbarity of war. Mark knew all too well — in war, nobody, especially the bad guys, followed the rules. Survival of the fittest was the name of the high-stakes games they played.

"Is the show still going to play?" Mark asked as Happy packed up their remaining gear and Mark put on his Barrett cap.

"The mission is still a go. These weren't the only terrorists to crawl out of the woodwork. Alpha Team came across another four-man team this morning in their area of operation too."

"This is some serious hardware for goat herders."

"You're right, brother. These rifles are 60 percent more powerful than your .50 Cal."

Mark and Happy moved the men and rifles into the hide, and removed tracks, scuffing and disturbances from the vicinity, making it appear as though no human had been there since the dawn of time. They geared up and moved with haste to their objective several kilometers away.

Walking downhill allowed them to move faster. The pre-planned route would put them on a ridge directly above the valley floor where the assault team would engage the convoy.

The operation had already kicked off by the time Bravo Team made it to their objective. The convoy of trucks had moved into the target area early. Mark and Happy moved into position and set up quickly.

# Chapter Twelve
## Camp Leatherneck Command Center
### Wednesday, October 8th, 0746 Hours

The colonel walked into the command center after his morning satellite briefing with the Pentagon. "What do we have, boys?" he asked with concern, as he saw the real-time image from the drone over the target area, showing a convoy of trucks on the large screen.

"The convoy has entered the AO early, sir. They're 12 minutes out," said a civilian contractor sitting behind a computer terminal, with a reflection of the screen on his glasses.

"Are all teams in place?"

"Zulu Team is the only one who hasn't responded to radio calls since they reached their waypoint last night, sir," said the Marine captain on the far left of the room near the radio.

"Any new developments about the four-man insurgent teams arriving in most areas?" Col. James asked.

"From what we can tell, Colonel, the insurgents knew approximately where our sniper teams would be, but luckily arrived after most of them were already hunkered down for the night. Intel confirmed the insurgents had weapons and resources capable of taking our teams out," a Marine sergeant reported from across the room.

The colonel examined a map of the area of operation and the sergeant explained to him that the enemy had positioned themselves behind where most of the sniper teams were located while covering the assault team on the valley floor. The captain explained more details.

"Son of a bitch!" the colonel yelled.

"The Afghans at this checkpoint in the mountains either took the morning off or were paid to let the trucks through, the captain continued. "We believe this is why the convoy is moving in early."

"I want the QRF to load up and head out, now! I want them to be ready for a fight if this goes south. There could be more enemy combatants we aren't aware of hiding out there."

"Roger that, sir," replied the captain relaying the order to the QRF team leader.

"Sir," said another Marine by the monitors. "The assault of the convoy is about to commence."

Everyone in the room gathered around the large screen to watch the ground team assault the convoy. The room remained silent, except for the nervous clicking of a pen and the hum of the air conditioners.

Bravo Team began to set up as charges were detonated in the area below, stopping the lead and rear truck of the convoy, according to the plan. The sounds rumbled through the valley, breaking the silence of the still morning as a firefight ensued. The assault force closed in on the trucks. Dozens of insurgents armed with AK-47s and light, belt-fed PKM machineguns dismounted the remaining trucks and engaged. The assault force was outnumbered four to one as the cracking sounds of the small arms echoed through the rocks.

Operators engaging the insurgents were flanking the trucks, enveloping from three sides as the battle gained intensity. Exploding grenades sent dust clouds into the air, taking down multiple enemy combatants at once. They were answered with rocket-propelled grenades from the other side, inflicting damage on the assault force and slowing their advance.

"Give me range and targets," Mark said as he opened the bipods and flipped open the scope covers on the Barrett .50 BMG rifle he had assembled, then turned his hat around. They hadn't had time to put on their Gillie suits, or properly camouflage the area, which left them exposed, but they had to move fast in order to assist their brothers in arms below.

Mark took a few long, slow, deep breaths to calm his heart rate, then started taking half breaths. He sat behind a rock in a crevasse they had found. He put his back to another rock and moved into place with his elbows on his knees, connecting bone to bone for more support. Mark settled behind the scope, a Nightforce

12-42-mmX56. He needed the large magnification for the long shots he frequently took. The over-sized objective, pulling each ounce of the surrounding light from the morning sun, made the battle taking place in front of him come to life, bright and bold. An action-packed drive-in, movie-screen moment unfolded as he prepared to engage.

"I sure hope Delta Team took their insurgent team out, if they had one on their side," Happy said as he set up the spotting scope.

"We'll find out soon enough, brother." Mark pulled out his dope chart for his scope as Happy ranged the targets. Elevation, temperature, barometric pressure, angle — it all had to be factored in before taking a shot.

Mark pulled back the large charging handle on the right side of the receiver, putting a round in the chamber of the rifle, as Happy called out the readings from his rangefinder. "Range: 800 meters, wind: quarter value. Push three left, machine-gun squad in the open, fire when ready."

"I see 'em," Mark replied calmly as he flipped the safety selector to fire. He took a breath and slowly let it out while pulling the slack from the trigger. The trigger broke, sending the bullet to its intended target and the butt of the rifle into his shoulder as it recoiled.

Happy continued to call out information, but Mark tuned him out and knew by instinct what to look for as Happy's voice faded into background noise. He hit each of the targets he aimed at and didn't lose momentum even when he reloaded the large 10-round magazines. They were not only a team, they were a unit — a well-oiled machine that relied on each other completely.

Happy called "hit" each time an enemy insurgent fell and kept calling out targets to Mark, who continued to fire, sometimes hitting more than one man at a time with the large bullets, which ripped through soft tissue and bone alike.

The men from the assault force were starting to dwindle as the battle raged. Mark knew an enemy sniper was out there somewhere, and he started to inflict damage on the U.S. forces.

"Happy, find the shooter," Mark yelled as he maintained a steady rate of fire on the insurgents below.

A bullet impacted close to them as Happy scanned the ridge on the far side of the valley with his spotting scope. It hit a rock in front of their position and exploded, sending shrapnel flying. A chunk cracked the lens on the rifle scope, but it still worked and Mark continued to engage the enemy.

"I see him," Happy reported as more rounds disintegrated the rocks around them. "Range: 2,200 meters. Wind: half value..."

Another round impacted even closer. They instinctively ducked, dodging rock fragments.

"I see him now," Mark said. "I need you to distract him. Get up and run to our left."

"You got it, brother."

Happy stood up to move as another round impacted the rocks, even closer still, sending chunks at him, cutting his right hand and face past the corner of his mouth. He continued to move as rounds appeared to follow him. Mark adjusted his scope slightly and fired his first round. Seeing where it impacted, as it hit a tree to the man's left, sending splinters into the air, he quickly adjusted his aim through the scope and fired again. This time he saw the familiar puff of pink mist in the distance.

Happy moved back to their position and Mark resumed shooting the insurgents attacking the assault force as the sound of helicopters began to resonate through the valley like war drums calling clans to battle.

# Chapter Thirteen
## Above the Valley
### Wednesday, October 8th, 0822 Hours

A woman's soft, but commanding voice came over the radio.

"Comanche, this is Snakebite, entering your AO. Would you boys like some assistance down there?"

"Snakebite, this is Comanche. We're under heavy enemy attack from all sides and taking sniper fire from the ridge above. Requesting immediate close air support on both sides of the convoy. Marking targets now."

"Roger that, Comanche. I see red smoke."

"I popped red smoke, engage at will. Danger close. Comanche out," she heard, barely audible above machine-gun fire, explosions and yelling.

"This is Snakebite. You boys find some cover down there. We are inbound hot."

The two attack helicopters flew low and fast into the valley, following each other as the ground came to life around the trucks. The 20mm, M197 three-barreled

Gatling nose-cannons from each aircraft clawed at the ground like hungry lions taking down antelope as they fired a fast strafing run.

Two trucks exploded in fire balls as the Cobras flew over. The blast waves knocked down insurgents on both sides of the vehicles like bowling pins flipping on end as a ball hits a strike. Plumes of dirt and smoke spiraled into the air. The birds made a quick orbit of the area, looking for more targets, then started firing in Mark and Happy's direction as they came back around.

Happy quickly swapped radio frequencies to talk to the Cobras as the rocks around Bravo Team exploded. "Cease fire, cease fire," he yelled. "You're firing on friendly forces."

"Indentify — call sign and position," said the woman pilot's voice as the helos stopped firing and peeled off.

"This is Bravo Team. Codename, Apache. We are at objective Tucson providing sniper cover for the assault team below. We encountered an enemy sniper on the adjacent ridge and have taken him out. How copy over?" Happy said.

Moments later the radio came back to life. "Sorry, Bravo Team. We have confirmed your identity and location. Keep up the good work. Snakebite out."

Most of the enemy combatants lay dead as the QRF flew into the area to assist the Cobras continuing their fly over of the vicinity. The exuberance of the battle started to wind down. Mark and Happy could see the men running out of the aircrafts once they touched down near what remained of the convoy. Bravo Team stayed in position to provide overwatch for the men on the ground as the medevacs flew in. The last of the enemy forces had laid down their weapons in surrender, as the remaining members of the assault force and QRF moved in.

The chaos unfolded on the screen for the men inside the command center. The mission wasn't playing out as it had been orchestrated. There were more enemy combatants than expected, Delta Team wasn't in position and couldn't be raised on the radio. Sniper fire from the opposite ridge, being Delta's side, pinned down Bravo Team, as well as the men in the ground assault team. Friendly forces were being hit hard until the Cobra attack helos entered the area and started firing into the mix on the ground.

The drone overhead provided a birds-eye view of the valley. The men could only watch in horror as their fellow Americans could be seen falling from the enemy's weapons.

As quickly as it started, the engagement ended.

"What the hell happened?" the colonel asked, looking around for answers.

The Marines and civilian technicians in the room continued to do their jobs, ignoring the ranting of the colonel.

The operators on the ground had performed to the best of their abilities from what the men in the communications room could see.

Picking up the pieces and figuring out how the mission had gone so terribly wrong could take days, if not longer.

"I expect a complete rundown of exactly what the hell went wrong by 1400 today," the colonel barked, walking out of the control room and slamming the door behind him.

# Chapter Fourteen
## The Valley
### Wednesday, October 8th, 0852 Hours

"Apache, this is Cherokee, over," came a voice on the radio,

"Go ahead, Cherokee," Happy replied.

"Mission is complete. Make your way down to the valley floor for your extract. They're expecting you."

"Roger that. Apache out."

"How's your face?" Mark asked Happy.

"What do you mean?"

"I'm assuming that's your blood?"

Happy raised his bloodied hand to his cheek. He pulled it away and looked at the thick crimson color on it.

"I believe you're in shock brother," Mark told him. "You better sit down while I look at those wounds."

Happy took a seat on a large, flat rock nearby. Mark pulled out his field medical kit to treat his teammate. He remained calm while Mark flushed his face and hand with saline solution, which allowed him to better assess Happy's wounds. He had a long cut from either a rock chip or bullet fragment that had nearly sliced through his cheek. His hand had multiple abrasions but none were dire.

"I'm going to put this bandage on but you're going to need stitches when we get back."

"Is it bad?" Happy asked.

"Not bad. You might have problems eating, talking or smiling for a while, but other than those issues, you're good, bro."

Happy grimaced as Mark applied the bandage. After they had packed their gear, they made their way to the valley floor to link up with the remainder of the assault force and quick reaction force.

A Marine Special Operations, or MARSOC, team had fast roped in to look for Delta Team and assess the sniper that Mark had eliminated.

On the way down, Mark stopped and took a pouch out of his pack, opened it up and set it down carefully. The viper from the day before slowly slithered out and moved into some nearby alpine flora. Happy shook his head as Mark shrugged and reshouldered his pack.

The dust had settled but the smell of burnt gunpowder hung heavy in the cool morning air. Bodies, blood, weapons and shell casings littered the area through which Mark and Happy walked. The perimeter now comprised of the quick reaction force. Death and destruction covered the valley floor.

Happy recognized a few Marines from base but didn't stop to visit. They were extremely busy, and he could catch up later. Capt. Dan Rogers locked eyes with him and they gave a quick recognition nod.

Men were running around, and screams from numerous directions were drowned out by the sound of the engines as Mark and Happy closed in on the medevac helicopters.

"Let's get on a helo, brother," Mark said to Happy.

They walked up the ramp of a Chinook in the nick of time. It lifted off before they could even find a seat.

The ride back on the helicopter was a surreal one as the men looked at their dead and wounded comrades surrounding them. Pools and streams of blood covered much of the deck of the aircraft. The lips of some of the wounded were moving. Others had open mouths, and Mark knew they were screaming, the sound drowned out by the overwhelming blare of the engines.

During their debriefing they were told the trucks had been empty except for insurgents. No crates had been recovered from the convoy. The mission had been deemed a failure in the eyes of the task force higher-ups.

"Our shipment made it over the border, boss," Nate relayed to Memphis as he walked into the little room.

"And the decoy convoy?"

"The plan worked. The Mujahideen retaliated for the unfortunate U.S. drone strike on their village last month and the taskforce is still stumbling around in the dark."

"How many Americans died for their country today?"

"Initial reports are six KIA and nine wounded, compared to 38 enemy combatants dead and five taken prisoner. We'll have them taken care of before morning, even though they pose no real threat."

"Good job, Nate. I knew there's a reason I keep you around. Send in Snake on your way out."

"Roger that, boss."

As Nate left the room Memphis sat behind his desk, a smile forming on his face.

"You wanted to see me, Commander?" Snake said, sauntering in, spitting tobacco into an old soda bottle.

"I've told you, son, rank is no longer necessary as long as you know your place. I need you to get me a secure video-conference with the house."

"But the next scheduled communication isn't for two more days."

"Don't make me repeat myself!"

"Roger that," Snake said, then spit into the bottle. "Your link should be active in a few minutes."

Snake left to go to the Comm Room and get the big boss on the line. Memphis flipped open the lap top on his desk, logged in and waited for the conference to begin.

Minutes later, a silhouetted picture could be seen, the screen displayed in color, an office with a desk by a large window and a blurry view of a lake. The bright room had colorful walls draped in blues, greens and yellows in an abstract design. A man with short blonde hair and a freshly shaved, chiseled face appeared behind the desk as the camera zoomed in, clearing the blurry image. He wore a black coat, white shirt and red tie. The blonde man sat as sound crackled. Moments later, Memphis could hear him.

"It's nice to see you, as always, Frank," said the man in the vibrant room. "Do you have good news for me?"

"Today's shipment made it over the border and is on its way to the facility."

"Excellent work. Are there any problems I should know about?"

"Nothing you should worry about. Everything's under control here."

"That's good to hear. And Frank, your replacement will be in country within two weeks. Your tours will overlap by one month before you rotate back to the states."

"Sir? I still have three months before my contract ends."

"Your expertise is needed elsewhere. We will discuss this further upon your return."

The transmission ended and the screen turned back to the screensaver of a tropical beach, with a palm tree in the background and a voluptuous brunette in a skimpy two-piece up front.

Memphis sighed and stared at his computer screen, contemplating what could be so important as to bring him home two months early. He and the other operators knew the cost of freedom. They had all been bloody in the mud too many times to count. The war on terror continued to be costly, and with the continuing changes to the rules of engagement from the current administration back home, they felt what they were doing had to be done, for God and for country.

# Chapter Fifteen
## Camp Bastion Flight Line
### Wednesday, October 8th, 1003 Hours

From the air, Mark could see the emergency response vehicles approaching the landing zone, blue and red lights flashing.

"Looks like a party down there," Happy managed to say, holding the blood-soaked bandage on his face as he looked out his window.

"I hope the colonel made some headway with his investigation," Mark said. "The enemy knew exactly where we were going to be."

"I know what you mean, brother."

Four helicopters landed as the emergency vehicles rolled up to them. The ramps lowered and the EMTs ran to get the wounded. Energy fogged the confined space. Mark and Happy hung back until everyone else moved off the aircraft.

Col. James and a few men in suits were waiting for them after the last wounded Marine had been taken away on a stretcher.

"Déjà vu," Happy said.

"You're right, this is getting old," Mark replied.

They walked down the ramp and were escorted to a black SUV.

"What's with you spooks and black?" Mark said sarcastically.

"Mitchell," the colonel started as they entered the vehicle.

"No sir, I won't be quiet. Happy and I do our job and do it very well. I'm getting tired of this bullshit. I want answers, not more questions."

"He's right," said the man in the passenger seat as the vehicle sped away. "These two men have proven they are highly trained operators with a good metric for risk/reward. We need more people like them on our side. We still don't know where the breach in the task force is, but with their help, we'll find it."

"And you are?" Mark asked.

"The names Smith."

"And you?" Mark asked the driver.

"Smith," he replied.

Mark shook his head, swearing under his breath.

"Do you still suspect someone inside the task force?" Happy asked, diverting attention from Mark.

"Each time we believe we've found the perpetrator, something happens to them," the colonel said.

"We thought it had been one or both of the men in Delta Team," the first Smith said. "But they were both found this morning, two kilometers from their objective, decapitated. They did manage to take out at least three enemy combatants before they were killed. The team who had been sent in saw evidence of an intense firefight over a large area. They didn't go out easily."

"Answers that question," Mark said.

"What can we do to help?" Happy asked.

"You can start by telling us about the crates, Mitchell," Smith said, turning around and glaring a hole through Mark's Kevlar helmet.

"I'm not even sure they were the same type of crate. If I tell you, I have to remain anonymous. I'm no rat."

"We know you're not, Mitchell, but we need information so we can save lives."

On the ride back, Mark told the men about the crates he and Happy had seen in the dungeon.

"Based on my knowledge of Memphis, I can't see him being involved in killing Americans," Mark said.

"We won't know anything for sure until we investigate the men down there," said the Smith driving. "The air filtration system needs to be serviced. That will be our in. Don't worry about repercussions, Mitchell."

"In the meantime, we're putting you two on sniper duty attached to a Marine unit," the colonel said. "There's an extremely talented sniper out there targeting coalition personnel. I want you to take him out if the opportunity arises. Report to Capt. Rogers in the morning. Here are your orders."

Mark took the paper and looked it over before handing it to Happy.

"Operation Bounding Fury," Happy read. "What are the specifics of the mission?"

"All I know is you and Mark will be overwatch for the Marine elements on the ground and provide counter-sniper support, as well. Any other specifics will need to be given by Rogers," James told him.

The remainder of the ride was quiet. Once they pulled up to the task force headquarters, a man wearing sunglasses, a black suit and a loose-fitting navy blue tie met with James. Mark and Happy had seen him around. His hard face had always been expressionless. He made Happy nervous and Mark curious.

"What do you suppose his name is?" Mark asked. "Smith?"

They chuckled as James turned to them. "I want you two to drop your gear at The Pit and report for your debriefing in 20 mics," the colonel grunted as he left with the man.

Mark and Happy did as instructed and were back at the command center within minutes.

"Here are the bolts from the two Istiglal sniper rifles," Mark said, handing them over to James. "And here's what the round looks like. I grabbed a few for souvenirs."

"We lost some good operators today because of these monsters," the colonel commented, while looking at one of the 14.5x114 mm 988gr, armor-piercing incendiary rounds Mark produced.

"There much larger than my .50 BMG rounds."

"Like one of my cigars. All right, tell me about the four-man team you encountered on the mountain."

"All four primarily spoke Dari, but two of them also spoke Arabic from time to time and made references to Syria and Iran, but they sounded like locals, from their dialect," Mark said. "Once we applied pressure they admitted they were given intel that we would be there, but wouldn't tell us how. They were paid to do a job and didn't ask questions. Did you get anything out of the five prisoners?"

"They aren't talking," said a familiar voice.

The men turned to see Hans Richter from Charlie Team. Richter had earned a reputation as a fierce warrior among his peers. His tactical prowess and cunning rivaled anyone in the unit of highly trained operators. Richter had known the men from Delta Team for several years, having served together in the Kommando Spezialkräfte — Germany's most elite Special Operations Forces.

He had lost two countrymen that day and insisted on being in the room for interrogation of the prisoners, wanting to get to the bottom of how his brothers had been killed by unseasoned enemy combatants.

Before joining the task force, Delta Team had seen combat in the Balkans, Iraq and Afghanistan. The men were well versed in airborne operations, counter-insurgency, counter-terrorism, covert ops, hostage rescue, intelligence operations and unconventional warfare.

"Has there been any word on Zulu Team's fate?" Happy asked.

"They're still missing," Col. James replied. "We have teams looking for them, but considering what happened to Delta, we're not optimistic."

Zulu Team was two English operators. They had been prior Special Reconnaissance Regiment, the unit formed to gather intelligence and carry out surveillance operations for the war on terror. They had been a perfect fit for the antiterrorism task force.

"I'm going to continue questioning the prisoners, Colonel," Hans said, leaving the room.

"You men go get your wounds treated, prep for your mission tomorrow with the Marine unit and get some rest," the colonel told Mark and Happy.

Screams rang out as they left the building.

# Chapter Sixteen
### Sniper Duty/Operation "Bounding Fury"
### Thursday, October 9th 0614 Hours

The 5-tons and HMMV convoy moved out early the next day for the upcoming night mission. The sign for Camp Leatherneck shrank in the rearview. The words below brought chills to anyone who read it.

*'Keep low, go fast. Kill first, die last. One shot, one kill. No luck, all skill.'*

Happy followed Mark's gaze and gave a low whistle. "That's right, brother. Words to live by."

Mark and Happy were accustomed to being flown in, or parachuting to their objective, but overwatch was overwatch, and this assignment should be a breeze with the aid of the large unit. They had been taken off the task force while the investigation continued.

"What rank are you guys?" a Marine sergeant sitting next to them in the Humvee asked.

"We're civilians," Happy told him.

"I don't get it, why are you on this mission?"

"That's classified, Devil Dog," Mark chimed in.

Captain Rogers was the only one they answered to, and even he didn't have any true authority over them. Mark and Happy smiled at one another. The convoy rolled down the dusty desert road. Drifts of sand covered the road from time to time, but their rig ran right through them.

The dust clouds the vehicles produced coated everything in layers of brown and gray. Most wore goggles and something to cover their faces. The turret gunners had it the worst, but they had to be there, scanning what area they could see.

Happy received 10 stitches on his face and had been told to perform light duty for at least two weeks to recover from the wound. He figured riding in a Humvee and sitting behind a scope would be the lightest duty he could perform other than lying in his rack, and had told the Navy doctor as much.

The convoy headed southeast toward Lashkar Gah, the capital of Helmand Province. The drive from the remote desert base usually proved uneventful until you moved closer to the population centers and colorful bazaars. IEDs were sometimes encountered on the desert road, but the insurgents had nowhere to hide after detonation. Detonating one near buildings, gave them a greater chance of getting away.

Chatter between the vehicles was kept to a minimum, but situation reports were relayed constantly to the Tactical Operations Center. The mission had satellite tasking, drone reconnaissance and an AWACS aircraft.

Once they moved closer to the city, radio traffic became heavy. There had been an explosion near a shopping center where another Marine unit had been patrolling. Medevacs could be heard flying overhead. They were seen landing in a field outside the rural areas not long after. Even from a distance the rotor wash had enough force to knock down clothes lines and scatter trash.

Out the window of the Humvee, pedestrians, bicyclists and horse-drawn wooden carts moved about near the site of the explosion, as if nothing out of the ordinary had happened.

"Stop the vehicle!" Mark yelled.

The driver looked at Capt. Rogers, who looked back at Mark and said over the radio, "This is Barracuda actual. Stop the convoy and watch our flanks."

The brakes were applied slowly so each vehicle had ample time to keep their dispersion.

Mark stepped out before the Humvee came to a stop and made his way to two Marines fighting with a German shepherd. One of them had a stick, the other a leash.

The gunners on top of the vehicles pointed their Browning .50 cals and Mk 19, 40mm, belt-fed grenade launchers out and scanned the hostile area.

"Schnell, *gyere ide*," Mark said loudly, remembering the Hungarian commands Dan used with her. Schnell stopped barking and ran over, her tongue flopping out the side of her mouth.

The two Marines stared at Mark in bewilderment and walked over to him and the dog.

"What are you doing with this canine and where's her handler?" Mark asked them.

"We were told to come out here and retrieve a dog, sir," said one of the men, with MP on his shoulder.

"Who told you to come get her?"

"A Lt. Walker," said the other MP, pointing toward a group of men.

Mark walked toward the group of Marines standing near a cluster of Humvees, Schnell by his side. "Lt. Walker!"

"I'm Lt. Walker," said a short and stocky Marine in full tactical gear.

"Where is Staff Sgt. Dan Brody?"

"Who are you?"

"I'm Mark Mitchell. Brody's a friend of mine. Now, where is he?"

Schnell nuzzled Mark's hand.

"Was he the explosive ordnance tech?" asked a Marine walking up to the growing group.

"What happened?" Mark demanded.

"Who are you, again, and what's your rank?" Lt. Walker asked Mark.

"Mark Mitchell and my rank is GS-12. Are you satisfied LT? I'm not here to make any waves, I just want to know where my friend is."

"What's a GS-12?" another Marine asked.

"It's a civilian rank equivalent to a major," Walker answered.

Capt. Rogers approached.

"Mitchell, what the hell's going on?"

"This is my friend's dog and no one will tell me where he is."

"He's dead," said a young private. "He was disarming another IED and he was vaporized."

A sergeant smacked the young Marine on his Kevlar helmet and glared at him.

The other Marines were silent as Mark looked down at Schnell, who whimpered.

"Let's go, girl," Mark told the German shepherd.

"You can't take her, sir," said the smaller MP.

"Watch me, Marine," Mark replied.

"I need to put a name in my report, who should I say...?"

"Mark Mitchell," said a few of the Marines in unison.

Mark and Schnell entered the Humvee, followed by Capt. Rogers.

"Is Dan...?" Happy started.

Ignoring the unspoken remainder of the sentence, Mark sat with a solemn look on his face and gave his full attention to Schnell.

The convoy continued to the rally point of the operation and began setting up for what they hoped would bring in a couple of high-ranking insurgents.

Mark would later read the report of what had happened to his friend.

Dan had been disarming a VBIED after being called to the scene by the grunt unit on patrol. A few decoy bombs had been seen, which had brought the Marines to the area to begin with. A working dog had been requested to identify the real ones from the decoys. Once Schnell located a device in the vehicle, Dan got to work. As was his habit, Dan wasn't wearing a suit.

"If these bombs are going to go off, it won't matter if you have a suit on or not. There won't be much of you left to worry about. Besides, it's hot and heavy. I can work faster without the damn suit on," he would say.

The insurgent who had planted the bomb inside a broken-down Toyota Corolla, must have seen that Dan was about to disarm the explosive. Right as Dan was about to cut the last wire, the vehicle exploded with so much force the shockwave threw the surrounding Marines back and to the ground, wounding some of them. Humvees 200 hundred yards away rocked from the force of the explosion. Old artillery shells left over from the Russian occupation of the 1980s were being used in more explosions across the country. From the force of this blast, more than a few were likely to have been used, as nearby buildings were also damaged.

A Marine on security saw a man, later identified as the bomber, running away from the scene and shot him. A cell-phone and a camera were found next to the body. Dan had been avenged, but that didn't make it any easier. Schnell would be kenneled and shipped back to Germany to be put with another handler, or retired. Mark planned on asking a favor of the colonel and hoped he'd able to keep his friend's dog.

Schnell had led over 300 missions in Iraq and Afghanistan with Dan Brody as her handler. She had sniffed out IEDs on numerous occasions and saved countless lives. She had been considered a hero by the men with whom she served over the years. When she patrolled with a Marine unit, they knew they would be safe from harm. One of numerous military working dogs in the country, Schnell served alongside the grunts on the ground. It was Mark's new mission to make sure she would be taken care of.

# Chapter Seventeen
## Sniper Duty / Night OPS
### Thursday, October 9th, 2336 Hours

The company had settled in for the night in a hasty circle of vehicles in a field. Patrols had been sent out in the outlying vicinity while fire teams watched the city from rooftops, covering the main force below. To the locals, the Marines looked like any other that had conducted night operations in the area. After 1800 hours, the call signs of the operation took effect.

"Sandman, this is Nighthawk. Sitrep, over."

"Nighthawk, this is Sandman. All's quiet in the hood."

The Marine unit on patrol east of the rally point of vehicles maneuvered toward the target building on foot. Humvees would be sent in after the raid kicked off so they didn't alert anyone prematurely.

Mark and Happy were on an adjacent rooftop 500 meters away listening to radio traffic and scanning the area of operation. Both had their SCAR 17s fitted with night vision/thermal scopes and suppressors. The suppressors would allow them to use the night vision without the muzzle flash and hide their positions better. With the short distance to most targets in the urban setting, the smaller round would do perfectly fine. The Barrett .50 cal Mark normally used would be overkill for the shooting they would be conducting.

"The sniper's out there man!" Mark whispered to Happy via com-link. "I can sense it in the air."

"I agree, it's too quiet."

"At least there's not a full moon and a clear sky tonight."

"What is it, a crescent moon? I can't tell with the scattered clouds."

"I believe so. I hope this works in our favor, and not his, brother."

The Marine unit, codenamed Sandman, closed in on their target building right after 2400 hours, the same time their backup team, Vertigo, moved into place. Nighthawk, the tactical command center's call sign for the operation, could see the whole process from above. The locals who were still awake and saw the Marines moving scurried into the buildings and houses that dotted the winding streets.

The pale glow of the moon through the clouds barely provided enough light to aid the teams as they silently moved through the shadows of the buildings. Sandman was about to breach the structure when the lights turned off inside. Mark grabbed the button on his com-link to call them off as they breached the front and side door. The whole city appeared to come to life. Smoke trails from RPG rounds mixed with tracer fire lit up the night sky like fireworks on New Year's Eve. Explosions rocked the target building as the Marines tripped booby traps on their way in.

The radio filled with screaming. Through the chaos, radio communication became difficult to understand. Humvees converged on the building to assist but were hit simultaneously by multiple RPGs. Mark and Happy were attempting to engage targets but several of the insurgents were using hit-and-run guerrilla techniques.

"I can't tell who's who down there," Happy said to Mark. "I'm switching to thermal."

"Roger that," Mark replied. "We need to displace soon. If the sniper's out there, he'll be picking us off pretty Ricky-Tic."

Mark and Happy grabbed their packs and moved out separately to their right and left flanks. They would be able to cover the assault team better and locate the sniper.

Mark swapped radio channels as he moved. "Nighthawk, this is Hit Man, I've activated the IR strobe on my helmet. Can you give me targets using thermals? Scan the area around the target building up to 1,500 meters in all directions."

"Roger that Hit Man. We see you and are scanning now."

The drone overhead sent real-time thermal images back to the TOC on an eight-second delay. The bird'-

s-eye view would allow them to locate hostiles more easily than Mark and Happy could from their rooftop vantage points.

Mark swapped frequencies momentarily. "Hit Man 2, this is Hit Man," he said to Happy.

"Go ahead Hit Man."

"Activate your IR strobe for the TOC to see. They're scanning the area for hostile heat signatures and are going to give us targets accordingly."

"Roger that, turning it on now and switching channels to the TOC."

Mark swapped back over, as well, and could hear Happy give the operations center his information.

Mark scanned the channels in between shooting. The radio chaos gradually improved as the firefight in the streets slowed down.

"Hit Man, this is Nighthawk. We show an unknown due west of your location. He's on a rooftop about 1,100 meters out and is firing on the assault force. He's hidden extremely well and must be using something to cover his muzzle from flash. He looked like any other warm body until we saw the muzzle heating up on his rifle. How copy, over."

"Looking now, Nighthawk," Mark replied. "I can't see him. I'm displacing for a better vantage point."

Mark flipped his night-vision monocular down at the front of his helmet and looked for higher ground.

The buildings were so close together that Mark could move over the rooftops about as fast as he could have on the ground. The command center guided him closer to the shooter while Happy continued to engage targets of opportunity.

Mark maneuvered within 400 meters when a hanging plant in front of him exploded.

"Taking fire, taking fire," he radioed after he dove for cover. "Did anyone see where the shot came from?"

"It's the same shooter Hit Man," said the voice on the TOC channel. "Hit Man 2, can you see Hit Man?"

"Roger that," Happy said.

"The shooter is 400 yards due north of his position."

"I still don't see him, Nighthawk."

"I do," Mark said over the radio.

Mark had low-crawled to the next roof and could see the heat signature of the shooter and the rifle's glowing barrel from the closer distance. He shot one round and saw the shooter roll over. The shooter started to get up. Mark put three more rounds in him.

"Target neutralized," Mark said over the net. "Send in a Marine element to secure the building. Hit Man 2, let's go see what we have."

"Roger that, Hit Man. On the way, forthwith."

The Marines established a perimeter around the original target building and the building the sniper had been in as helicopters flew in to support the men on the ground. Sporadic shooting could still be heard on in the streets between the insurgents and Marines. The attack had left a few Marines dead or wounded, and the rest on edge.

"What do we have, Captain?" Mark inquired as he walked toward the building.

"Unknown, but the shooter appears to have been alone. There's a team on the way to figure out if this is the same guy who's been killing our men."

"Roger that, Captain. Do you mind if we go take a look?"

"Go ahead, but don't touch anything."

Mark and Happy walked up the stairs. On the roof, they could see why the sniper had picked the location. He had a perfect view of the target building and the rest of the city for over 2,000 meters.

"How did he know this mission was happening?" Happy asked.

"Good question, brother," Mark replied. "How did he know about any of the recent missions?"

"I want to find out who this guy is," Happy said, turning on his red-lens flashlight.

"Be quick about it."

Happy began searching the man. "No wallet, go figure. Scars and tattoos, though. Well, this is interesting. Help me roll him over."

They rolled the man onto his back. Happy pulled up the man's shirt.

"Someone's coming," Mark whispered and rolled the man back to the position in which they had found him.

He and Happy moved a few feet away and pretended to look from a distance as others approached the scene.

"Who the hell are you two and what are you doing up here?" demanded a man, dressed in black from head to toe and shining a bright flashlight on them.

"We're the snipers attached to the Marine company," Happy told him.

"Which one of you killed this man?" he asked.

"I did," Mark replied.

"Good job. Now, I'd like you men to leave so we can figure out who he is and why he's been targeting coalition personnel."

"Roger that," Mark said.

They stopped at the bottom of the stairs before exiting the structure.

"Did you find anything?" Mark asked Happy.

"He's Russian, SPETSNAZ GRU, and he had a few prison tattoos. I'm betting he had been a mercenary working for the highest bidder. I saw quite a few scars from knife wounds and bullet holes and his back showed signs he had been whipped. The back tattoo looked distorted and cut up. The guy saw some shit in his day."

"Interesting," Mark commented. "But what does it mean?"

The area crawled with Marines while helicopters flying search patterns filled the sky over the city.

The operation had been another set-up. Eight Marines had been killed by the blasts and the rooftop sniper. More men would've been killed if Mark hadn't acted quickly in taking out the sniper.

The streets were littered with shell casings from AK-47s, M4s and light machine guns from both sides.

Two of the up-armored Humvees were disabled from the RPG attacks, but no one inside had been badly hurt. Bruises and lacerations were the worst injuries any of the men had received. The RPGs hits had spiderwebbed or shattered most of the windows in each vehicle. Tires lay shredded near the rigs, one still smoldering after catching on fire.

Dawn approached. Most of the men had been up for over 24 hours, and it showed.

Mark walked to the rig in which Schnell had been, waiting for his return. She whined with excitement as he let her out to relieve herself. She came back to Mark after checking the area. He gave her well-deserved attention while they waited for their orders.

The patrols were called in and the convoy left the city smaller than it had arrived.

The mystery of the Russian sniper weighed heavily on Mark and Happy. This wasn't the first time a heavy hitter had been found among the dead.

# Chapter Eighteen
Camp Leatherneck
Friday, October 10<sup>th</sup>, 0844 Hours

Mark and Happy were dropped off at their barracks.

"Thanks for a great evening on the town, Captain," Happy said with a half smile, due to his wound and the mission's outcome.

"My pleasure, men," Rogers replied.

"Yeah, we'll have to do it again sometime," Mark commented. "And, Captain, sorry about your men."

Rogers nodded, not needing to say anything else.

Mark and Happy walked through the main door of The Pit and heard blaring music. Lynyrd Skynyrd's "Sweet Home Alabama" filled the room. Happy smiled as usual and started dancing on the way in while Schnell stopped, cocked her head and stared at him. Mark shook his head and told Schnell, "Yep, he is a strange one, girl."

They put up their weapons and gear and strolled over to the female showers to wash up. Being midmorning, no one was around. This wasn't their time to use the facilities, according to the sign on the entrance, but they sauntered in anyway and showered quickly, hoping not to cause any grief among their counterparts. Once done, they snuck back out, avoiding female encounters. They headed to their separate rooms to get some much-needed sleep before reporting for duty again. Mark made up a blanket into a bed for Schnell, onto which she immediately curled, and they quickly fell asleep.

Mark woke to heavy knocking. His reflexive jerk to the nightstand accidently knocked the light over, breaking the bulb on the floor. Reaching under his pillow, he grabbed his 1911 .45 ACP and switched on the LED light attached to the rail under the barrel. The knocking intensified as Mark rubbed his face in his palms. Schnell stood near the door with her tail stiff and pointed.

"Alright, damn you, I'm coming!"

Mark moved to the side to avoid stepping in the broken glass on the plywood deck of his room. He reached up and moved the 2-by-4 that served as a lock. Happy stood outside with his half-smile beaming at Mark.

"Let's go, sunshine," Happy said, looking down at Mark's smiley-face boxers.

"Go where, and what time is it?"

"It's a few minutes after 1800 hours and time for a beer," Happy said cheerfully while flipping on the lights in the room.

"Have you talked to the colonel yet?" Mark dressed in tan khaki pants, a blue-and-white Hawaiian shirt and his Barrett cap.

"Are you really wearing that?"

"Uh, yeah. Its Friday, isn't it?"

Happy shook his head as Mark cleaned up the glass, filled Schnell's food bowl and told her he would be back in a while. They left the barracks for Duke's.

"Yes, I've talked to the colonel," Happy said. "And no, he doesn't need to see us until tomorrow."

"Do we have another mission?"

"I don't know, just show up at 0800. We should find out then."

At the aid station they could see people walking down the stairs to the pub as was typical for a Friday night. Work schedules were not often the typical Monday through Friday, so those lucky enough to have a weekend took full advantage of it. As Mark and Happy made their way to the bowels of the medical center, the room appeared to be near capacity. The sound of techno music filled their ears even before getting all the way in. Mark checked his handgun and knife at the door. He scanned the place. Not seeing anyone he really wanted to visit with, he and Happy made their way to the bar. Duke looked slammed and had a couple of people helping him behind the bar.

"What can I get you guys?" Duke asked.

"The usual is fine," Mark told him.

Duke grabbed the beers and a shot of tequila for Mark. He pointed and asked Happy, "You need a straw?"

"No, I'm good. It was just a graze."

Duke smiled and winked. Mark paid for the drinks. He and Happy sauntered toward the billiard tables while a man called a pocket, pulled back his stick and sent the cue ball clanking into his last stripe. Mark didn't like to play when there were so many people, but for Happy, the more, the better. He would challenge anyone, moving like a great white shark in a lagoon full of minnows.

Mark took a seat on a stool by the wall and relaxed while watching the room. There was a game of darts going, men were flirting with women and vice versa. A few couples were making out in booths or on the dance floor. As usual, a haze of cigarette and cigar smoke blanketed the room like fog on a cool morning. Mark could only take the second-hand smoke for so long before feeling an overwhelming urge to get some fresh air, even with the overhead fans on high.

A couple of beers later a scuffle broke out by the dance floor. Mark watched Duke wave at the door bouncers to go investigate. It's normal for a Navy guy and a Marine to get into it. The Marine would call the sailor a squid or the Marine would be called a jarhead. Usually, the fight would end after being broken up. Duke would buy the men a round and everything would go back to normal. This time, however, behemoth petty officer who started the argument wouldn't back down, even when the equally large bouncers became involved. Blows were thrown and the fight started to spread among the other patrons as people knocked into each other.

Each time Mark approached the instigator a group of sailors shoved Mark backward while cheering on their comrade. Determined to help Duke before the MPs were called and the place shut down, Mark called out the giant of a man, which prompted him to become the target. Mark started to second guess helping as the man advanced, looking even larger than he did across the room.

Before Mark knew it the mountain had his left hand around Mark's throat and he knocked Mark's Barrett cap off. The sailor lifted Mark off the ground with the single hand. Legs dangling, Mark slapped both of the sailor's ears. He howled in pain and let Mark go. Mark caught his breath as a large boot swung his way. He put his hands together to block the blow. As they connected, the momentum sent Mark flying backward into the wall.

The dartboard fell and slammed onto his head. He jumped to a kneeling stance and tried to focus. A scrawny man next to him who had been hiding under a table grabbed a handful of darts and started throwing them. Not being especially good at this particular game, most of them missed the large target in front of them. One finally caught the sailor in the left arm and another in his right leg. This made him angrier.

Mark appreciated his efforts but pushed the man out of the way and grabbed the only other available item, throwing the dartboard like a Frisbee. The thick chunk of wood caught the attacker in the gut, making him double over in pain. Mark ran toward the giant, kicked his right knee, sent a palm into his chest and an elbow across his face. Mark finished him off with a head butt to the nose. The colossus fell with a thunderous noise. Silence filled the room as Duke made his way over.

He handed Mark his hat. "I knew you could handle yourself Mitchell, but I had no idea you were such a badass!"

"I'm getting too old for this shit," Mark managed, catching his breath and holding his throat.

Duke slapped him on the back, making Mark grimace in pain. The crowd started picking the place up and the music came back to life.

A random Marine bought Mark a beer for his heroism. "Nice shirt," he said with a smile.

"Are you mocking my shirt?" The man made a hasty exit.

Mark would soon follow, quickly finishing the beer and telling Happy he was taking off. He collected his weapons and started back to his room. Walking by the command center, he saw a single light through a second-floor window and went inside to investigate.

A door halfway down the corridor had been left ajar. He paused to listen for a moment. As unobtrusively as he could, Mark walked in. Sandy, with her back to the door, stood by a Xerox machine copying documents, unaware of his presence.

"Whatcha doing there, lady?" Mark asked when he moved closer.

Sandy spun around with a Glock in her right hand, which Mark grabbed with his left and pulled her close.

"Whoa there, darlin'! I didn't mean to scare you."

"I'm sorry, Mark. It's a normal reaction to being scared half to death."

Mark inhaled, taking in the sweet smell of her intoxicating perfume.

"No, I'm sorry," Mark said, letting her go but not the gun. "I saw a light and came up to see if it was left on by accident. What do you have this for?"

"Doesn't everyone?" she asked, pointing at Mark's leg holster and sidearm.

"You're right. Dumb question." Mark handed her Glock back and sat on a table behind him.

"I was finishing up some paperwork for the colonel and then I was headed to Duke's. Would you care to join me, or...?"

Sandy approached Mark at the table, sliding her hands up his thighs. He matched her short height when he sat. Mark was about to reply when she leaned forward, took off his hat and kissed his open mouth before words could be formed. Surprised, Mark didn't skip a beat. He slid to the edge of the table, pulling her close as their kiss deepened.

Sandy leaned into him, indicating her intentions. She unbuttoned his Hawaiian shirt and slid it down his muscular arms, kissing his chest and biting his left nipple, making him tense up. Mark pulled her tight shirt over her head and kissed her again. She stepped back and smiled as she unbuttoned her pants. She moved back into position in front of him, her heavy breathing making her breasts heave. Their kiss continued long and deep again as Sandy started to unbuckle his belt. Mark grabbed the clasp on the back of her bra with his left hand and unhooked it with one fluid motion, making her gasp. Mark grabbed a fistful of her hair, tilting her head back. She moaned as he kissed her neck.

As Sandy unzipped Mark's trousers, half a dozen armed men burst into the room. She pulled Mark close, using him to cover her exposed chest.

"What the hell's going on?" Mark demanded.

One of the MPs had an ear-to-ear, shit-eating grin on his face.

The colonel walked in behind them, shook his head and scrunched his brow, obviously annoyed at the sight before him. "Mitchell, you need to get the hell out of here."

"Colonel, I know this isn't the place for this, but if you give us a minute, we'll clear out."

An MP approached as they dressed. "Cassandra Ackerman, you're under arrest for treason, conspiracy to commit murder and terrorism."

Mark shot the colonel a questioning look as another MP handcuffed Sandy. They escorted her out of the room without a word. Seconds later, Mark remained the only one there. He sat down in a high-back leather chair and shook his head in disbelief.

"OK, let me get this straight," Happy started, back in Mark's room. "You were about to break in that filly, and the colonel walked in on you?"

"Don't forget the six MPs," Mark added.

"What the hell did they arrest that sweet little girl for?"

"They said treason, conspiracy to commit murder and terrorism. The colonel left before I could find out anymore, but my guess is, he found the leak in the task force."

"Damn. That would make sense. I wonder if it's what the morning meeting is for."

"I'm sure we'll find out soon enough. Now get out of my room so I can nurse my blue balls in silence."

# Chapter Nineteen
**Baltimore, Maryland near Catonsville**
**Top floor of the Executive**
**Security building**
**Friday, October 10<sup>th</sup>, 1427 Hours**

"Mr. King, you have a call on line two," said a female voice through the intercom. "It's Mr. Ryland sir.

Concern crossed Thomas King's face. He stared out the large bay windows of his top-floor office. A large steel pole held a massive American flag, flapping in the wind, in the courtyard below. The security company he had built after leaving a decade-long career in the SEALs was flourishing, but it didn't come without its own set of troubles.

"Dennis," he said pushing the speaker phone button. "You better have some good news for me, because I've already had enough bad today."

"Go Packers."

Tom pushed a button and flipped a switch. If anyone had been listening, they would only hear one of numerous recorded conversations they had had about football games.

"The line is secure."

"I wish I did have good news, sir," said Dennis Ryland, his second in command. "The Russian is dead."

"Where are you, Dennis?"

"I'm in flight over the Atlantic, sir. I'll be arriving in a couple of hours."

"Good. We need to sit down with the board and discuss our options. The election is only days away."

"Roger that, sir."

Tom hit the end button, picked up a green Squeeze Ball and sat back in his brown leather chair. He knew from his days in the field that not all operations ran as smoothly as he would like, but too much hung in the balance right now. His vision for the future was shared by a number of people, not only in this country, but numerous others worldwide. Yet one of his operatives had been captured and one killed in less than 24 hours, and in the same theatre, no less.

Tom pushed a button on his phone. "Danni, have my truck meet me up front. I'm heading to the range."

"Yes sir, Mr. King," she said.

Tom pressed a panel into the wall. It opened up, exposing a large, hidden closet with clothing and tactical gear on one side and a row of weapons on the other. He slowly made his way to the end, considering the multitude of equipment as he began to undress. He hung up his suit and put on a change of clothes more appropriate for getting dirty — khaki pants and a short-sleeved t-shirt. Grabbing a vest with magazines adorning the front and a Sig Saur 556 short-barrel carbine, he left the room, hitting the panel to close the wall on his way out.

The range was the perfect place to blow off a little steam. If things got too bad with a mission, he would jump on one of his private jets and join a team in the field. To Tom, nothing came close to the adrenaline rush of real combat in a Third-World country.

Rod Sanchez was waiting for him when he walked off the elevator on the bottom floor. They walked to the black Chevy Suburban Rod had brought up from the lower level parking garage.

"Your instructions, sir?" He asked Tom as they started down Patriot Lane toward the Interstate.

"Let's go light some shit up," Tom said with a smile.

"Roger that."

Rod had been an Army Ranger for 12 years and one of the first operators who joined Executive Security after its inception. In his late 50s now, with streaks of gray hair, he was Tom's No.1 instructor and interrogator in CONUS. He very rarely left the continental U.S. for anything these days. He had already seen the world and was content with his current position.

"So, boss, I hear Memphis is coming home early?"

"Who told you?"

"It's the word around the house. The man is a legend, after all."

"He'll be back eventually, same as any operator who transitions from here to there."

"How's it going in country, BTW?"

"What the fuck is BTW?"

"By the way —, you don't text? It's all I can do to keep up with my grandkids."

"I speak English, Rod, and I expect the people around me to, also. This is still the land of the free and the home of the brave!"

"I didn't mean any disrespect, boss. We better bust some caps, huh? I packed a few extras for this range trip. I felt a little hostility on the phone with the Mrs."

"The Mrs.?"

"Yeah, your secretary — you're still hittin' that, aren't you?"

"Rod."

"Yeah boss?"

"Shut the fuck up."

Rod said no more. He'd heard rumors about an associate King had once worked with who sometimes talked too much. The way Rod heard it, they had gone fishing and no one ever heard from the man again. He didn't want to push his luck. He continued driving toward Interstate 695 and the private, 62-acre range and training grounds the company owned in Marriottsville.

Tom had originally wanted the whole facility on the same chunk of land, but the state fought him tooth and nail about the range. They didn't want the facility to be too close to the city. Marriottsville is only about 20 minutes away, but Tom wasn't happy about the whole scenario.

"We're about there, sir," Rod piped up.

"Take me by the main building. I want to see the new batch of recruits first."

"Roger that, sir."

A guard came out of the shack and put his hand up. Rod brought the vehicle to a stop and powered down the tinted window.

"How's tricks, Stacy?" Rod taunted.

"Oh, it's just you," the man said sarcastically.

"Actually, Mr. King's in the back and he wants to go shooting after we check out the cherries."

"Open the gate," Stacy Morgan told the other guard. Stacy had applied to Executive Security after eight years in the Air Force but didn't make the cut even after three attempts. He was offered a job as a gate guard and accepted it, to be close to the action.

The SUV drove through the complex's different areas so Tom could see the progress he usually only read about in reports from what he called, "The Ranch." He had recruited the best of the best to hire and train as operators the company would ship throughout the world to perform the duties for which each client paid good money.

Between the living quarters, office buildings and classrooms were obstacle courses and other training facilities. Beyond those buildings were ranges for handgun and rifle shooting and kill houses for urban warfare training, with gunfire heard day and night.

Before long, they were walking through the barracks and training grounds, looking at the new recruits.

They didn't stop to talk to anyone, but received looks and nods from instructors and trainees alike. Tom liked to occasionally see if his money was being put to good use. Most of the applicants had prior military service. Some came from law enforcement, and a few were ordinary, average, red-blooded Americans wanting to do his part — and be compensated greatly for it. Unfortunately, not many of the raw recruits made it through to graduation to move on to active service in the numerous combat units Executive Security had in play across the globe.

"All right, I've seen enough, Rod. Let's go blow off some steam."

They drove to the kill house first. Rod loved practicing with the boss. Who wouldn't enjoy an afternoon shooting free ammo on full auto while getting paid handsomely at the same time? He couldn't think of anyone.

The men geared up. After checking each other and putting their weapons into condition one, with rounds in the chambers, they entered the two-story, cinderblock building, heavily marked up with bullet holes. Immediately upon entering, reactive electro-mechanical and pneumatic pop-up targets appeared and the shooting began.

# Chapter Twenty

After breakfast at the chow hall, Mark and Happy made their way to the morning briefing. When they entered the building they noticed more people than usual scurrying in the corridors.

Walking into the designated room, the other operators were already in conversation. When they saw Mark, they started clapping, whistling and making comments like, "Do me on the colonel's desk next," and, "Look, it's the rodeo rider."

Mark shook his head and took a seat at one of the back tables. The colonel walked in with a tall, thin man with curly black hair.

"Alright, enough," he growled, while glaring at Mark. "This is Howard Spencer and he'll be taking Ms. Ackerman's place on the task force."

"What can you tell us about last night, sir?" One of the new British members asked while glancing in Mark's direction with a smirk on his face.

"Well..." the colonel cleared his throat. "Sandy, Ms. Ackerman, has been arrested and incarcerated. According to classified evidence, she was the leak in the task force. We're almost positive she acted alone, which means each of our pending operations have been given a green light by the powers that be. You will be very busy in the next few weeks."

"So, what exactly happened?" Valentine asked.

"The details are still under investigation and portions of it are likely to remain classified."

"And what should we call you, mate?" one of the other Brits asked Spencer.

"Who, me?" Spencer asked, pushing his glasses back onto the bridge of his nose.

"No, the little one in the school girl outfit — Yes, you, you wanker!"

"Um — well, as the colonel said, my name is Howard..."

"We all heard your bloody name. What should we call you on the radio?"

"How about Snake Eyes," Hans Richter put in.

"You mean because of his glasses?" Mark asked.

"Well, yeah."

"That's original."

"Do you have something better, Mitchell?"

"As a matter of fact..." Mark started, but the room erupted in men throwing out other names, arguing and laughing amongst themselves.

"Alright, damn you," the colonel boomed. "Snake Eyes is fine, thank you, Mr. Richter. Now, *all* of you sit down and listen up. We've heard more chatter about shipments of crates and believe we're close to a lead in the investigation."

The men gave their full attention to the colonel.

"Unfortunately, Hans wasn't able to get much out of the five captured enemy combatants we took from the ambush on the convoy. They somehow obtained some Kool-Aid and took their own lives before being questioned further."

"How did they get poison if they were incarcerated and searched before hand?" Happy wanted to know.

"Medical examination indicates someone tainted either their food or water before it was served to them in their cells. We're questioning everyone on duty at the time, from the cooks to the guards. At this time, Ms. Ackerman is denying any involvement, which could indicate a second mole, but evidence indicates she is lying. As the investigation is still ongoing, each one of you here needs to focus on the larger picture. Some of the intel we've gathered has pointed us in the direction of the Panjshir Valley, located south of the Hindu Kush Mountains of north-central Afghanistan, 150 kilometers north of Kabul. Mr. Spencer, if you please."

Spencer turned down the lights and flipped on the screen for a Power-Point. "As the colonel pointed out, there has been an unusual amount of activity in this area. Exactly what significance this holds, we still don't know. A plan is being devised to enter the area and assess any role the locals might have in aiding terrorists activities. You will be working in conjunction with the Afghan Armed Forces to gain the trust and cooperation of the locals and hopefully minimize civilian casualties if the operation goes awry."

The room exploded with questions and opposition to the Afghanis being involved. Known for their "flight-not-fight" doctrines when being shot at, many coalition troops' lives had been put in danger on various missions during collaborations in the past. The colonel quickly put an end to the discussions.

"Shut up!" he yelled. "I don't like this any more than you do, but this order comes from the top. We are here to help this country get back on its feet, and Washington wants the local military involved in more joint operations, especially when it comes to the country's resources. Like it or not, this is how it will be, gentleman. With any luck, this operation will commence in a few days. In the meantime, I have reconnaissance duties for Bravo and Charlie. The rest of you, get some rest and make sure your gear is packed and ready. Dismissed, gentleman."

The four men from Bravo and Charlie stayed behind, waiting for the last of the others to file out.

Mark looked at Happy. "How's your face, buddy? It's looking a little droopy."

"It's doing great. The stitches come out in a few days. It doesn't even hurt."

"OK," the colonel began, looking at the four men after the door was shut. "You men are going HALO in to separate peaks overlooking the target area before this joint operation commences. Because of the snow on the mountains of the region, you will need to take snowshoes and skis. You will be taking more gear than normal for the higher elevations, so if any of you have any doubt you will be able to accomplish your mission, I need to know sooner than later so I can replace you. Happy, how are your wounds healing?"

"I'm good to go, sir."

"Alright, men, get the list of essential gear and call signs from Spencer and start packing. You leave tonight and will be inserted under the cover of darkness."

# Chapter Twenty-One
## The Pit
### Saturday, October 11th, 1522 Hours

They would be jumping from 30,000 feet to be invisible to anyone who might be in the area. The men would be wearing full-face breathing apparatuses to avoid frostbite and hypoxia.

Mark, Happy, Hans and Günther from Charlie Team were in good spirits as they packed gear for the mission.

A night drop from such a high altitude with so much gear was risky enough, but to parachute in to a snow-covered peak was near suicide, especially conducting a high-altitude low opening, or HALO. The men would need to rely not only on their training, but a certain amount of luck as they came back to Earth. They didn't talk about it, but fear had to be factored in to a certain degree or the possibility of not making it back would grow expediently.

"Are you sure you're good to go?" Mark asked Happy.

"If I wasn't, brother, you'd be the first to know."

"Good enough for me."

Hans and Günther spoke in German while filling their packs and double checking they had everything they would need. They spoke English well, but spoke in their native tongue to each other and their other country-men.

Each team had their separate objectives and wouldn't be anywhere close to one another initially. If either team needed assistance, they would have to rely on the green machine to come to their aid. The mission had been deemed extremely high priority, and all available assets would be in play to achieve success.

Duke stopped by to pick up Schnell. He had agreed to watch her while Mark was out on missions. He noticed Mark's thoughtful mood and didn't stay around to chat.

Once the men had their gear ready they were taken to a hangar to prep their parachutes. The Marine Corps parachute riggers did a damn fine job, but Hans liked to pack his own. He had done this for years after he experienced a streamer malfunction with his main chute on a combat mission over the Balkans and barely had enough time to pull his reserve, once he cut away the main. He landed hard and walked away with only a sprained ankle, but it could've been much worse.

"Are you sure you don't want any help, buddy?" Mark taunted Hans inside the hangar.

"Nine!" he grunted. "I can do it myself."

Mark and Happy grinned at each other. Hans muttered profanity in German while packing the chute.

"Ain't life grand?" Happy said as they waited for their ride.

They were accustomed to the hurry-up-and-wait mentality of the military, but that didn't make it any better. Mark took advantage of the lax time to function check his weapons once more. He'd already done it twice, but a third time never hurt. Of all his gear, his weapons were the most significant.

Not long after dark they were told their ride to the C130 transport plane was ready. They were packed on a 5-ton truck with the aid of a couple of Marines, and were soon rolling down the flight line to board the aircraft.

The colonel was waiting by the ramp at the rear of the turbo prop.

"You boys ready?"

"I suppose we are," Mark replied.

He received a thumbs up from Happy and a grunt from Hans. Günther said nothing.

"Well all right then, I'm off to the comm room and will be monitoring your progress. Happy landing, gents."

Once they stowed their gear and were seated, the power plants started up and the ramp closed moments before taxi and takeoff.

# Chapter Twenty-Two
### Baltimore, Maryland
### Conference room of the Executive
### Security building
### The previous Day

"Gentleman, thank you for making this meeting on such short notice," Tom King started. "As some of you may already be aware, we've had some minor setbacks in Afghanistan. But, not to worry. We have it under control."

The half dozen suits sitting around the long, rectangular Bocote table were hanging on every word. The wood was one of the most expensive in the world, with dramatic brown and black strips in the grain. Tom imported it from Ecuador himself.

The board members at the table consisted of a U.S. senator from Montana, an oil tycoon from Brazil, a former Russian KGB operative and billionaire from Great Britain. The other two members were a former CIA station chief from Spain and a man whose background only Tom knew. Two more were attending via secure video conferencing. One of them, Hiroshi Nakamura, headed up the technology division. The other was a high-ranking member of the U.S. military they called the Admiral. They each had their specialties, making the gears of the company turn at a speed no other group could accomplish.

The large, flat screen at the front of the room came to life with images as Tom continued.

"As you know, the elections in Angola will take place next week. We anticipate a smooth transition."

"Are you certain of this?" the billionaire asked. He was wearing a black, tailored Jon Green suit and smoothed his short gray beard with a tiny comb before continuing. "There's no chance of a revolt or another civil war?"

"Our men have been on the ground for more than six months working with the Minister of Defense to make sure the country continues to stabilize out of the dark ages," Tom told them. "We stand to make an astronomical amount of money once the right man is in power. Not only will our operators remain gainfully employed, but our interests in the country's oil and diamond trades will prosper beyond your wildest dreams."

Tom took his seat at the head of the table while a petite young woman with long brown hair continued where he took off. Most of the men were watching her tight brown skirt clinching her hips as she walked.

"If you gentleman are having trouble focusing on the task at hand, maybe I should leave?" she asserted.

Her name was Katarina Vetrov. She was Russian-American, born in New Jersey, but she looked, sounded and held herself as if she came straight from the motherland. Katarina was intelligent, charismatic and incredibly well kept. She was a former NSA analyst and was exceedingly good at her job, which is why Tom had hired her.

"We're very sorry, young lady," said the senator, an older man with an abundance of wrinkles. "We try our best to be professional but, nonetheless, we're just a bunch of dirty old men."

She glared at Tom. "Mr. King, can you please control your board members?"

"My apologies, Ms. Vetrov," Tom said wholeheartedly as he looked around the room. "They will comply or can leave and get this briefing via email."

"Please continue, Ms. Vetrov," said Victor, in Russian. The former KGB officer gave the others a stern look.

"As I was saying," Katarina began again. "The operation in Afghanistan is running exceedingly smooth with few hiccups. One of our operatives was recently killed and another arrested, but we've covered our tracks well. Our operative working under the name of Cassandra Ackerman will be on a flight to Ramstein this afternoon. She will be picked up by our men once she lands and come back here for her debrief before she goes on her next mission."

"And what is her next mission?" the Brazilian asked.

"She will be joining the team already on the ground in Angola," Vetrov told him. "Her skills are invaluable to the company and we know she will be a perfect fit over there."

"Did the Russian accomplish his mission before he was terminated?" the senator asked.

"Unfortunately he didn't. One of his last targets took him down."

"Very unfortunate, indeed."

"How is the new batch of recruits coming along at the training center?" the CIA operative asked.

"I stopped there yesterday," Tom told him. "The rigorous selection process we've implemented is continuing to provide us with an 83 percent attrition rate, which is higher than any military special force on the planet, even the SEALs, which is at 75 to 80 percent currently. We have the best of the best, and I, for one, wouldn't have it any other way."

The men were impressed, nodding their heads in approval. Each knew their interests were being well cared for by Tom and his men.

"What about the antiterrorism task force on the ground in Afghanistan?" asked the mystery man on the board, taking a half-smoked Cuban cigar out of his mouth and exhaling smoke rings.

"What about it?" Katarina asked.

"I'm concerned they're getting too close to finding out what we're doing over there."

"The men I've selected and put in play in country, are doing a better job than expected and continue to show results," Tom said. "We've got nothing to worry about, as the Admiral can attest. I want to thank each of you for making an appearance. Ms. Vetrov, if you please."

The man remained persistent. "Did the Russian cover his tracks? Their investigation could tie all of the dead men together if they look in the right places."

"I assure you," Tom told him sternly. "It was handled discreetly. Ms. Ackerman played an incredibly large role in making sure they looked random. The Admiral is in country, as well, aiding our assets over there."

Katarina handed each man a large manila envelope as they left. She shut off the TV and computer and prepared to walk out.

Once the board members were gone, Rod Sanchez walked in, trailed by Dennis Ryland, who had recently arrived from overseas.

"Welcome back, Mr. Ryland," Katarina said with a smile as she passed the men on her way out.

"Rod I need you to get Memphis on a secure feed, right away," Tom said.

"Give me a few minutes, sir. Mr. King, is everything all right?"

"It will be soon enough." He turned to Ryland. "Dennis, we need to talk."

# Chapter Twenty-Three
### In Flight
### Saturday, October 11th, 2147 Hours

Charlie Team would be jumping first, so they were positioned near the rear of the aircraft. It took approximately an hour for the plane to reach the first drop zone.

A green light near the ramp somewhat brightened the dimly-lit belly of the plane, then turned off. The crew-members and the four men in the back donned their re-breathers in anticipation of the ramp lowering.

Hans and Günther stood once the cabin pressurized and the ramp lowered. Even with their cold-weather gear on, the men felt the near-arctic conditions of the high altitude. No lights could be seen out of the back of the bird. Only thick darkness, like they were peering into a black hole. Charlie Team moved slowly with their bulk of gear after checking each other again. The green light appeared again and they slipped away into the dark void in front of them, as if they had never been there.

Mark and Happy prepared themselves to do the same.

The aircraft banked slightly to the left, then leveled out. A few minutes later the crew chief motioned for Bravo Team to stand. They made their way to the ramp, gave each other and the chief a thumbs-up. They walked off the ramp once the green light shown on the bulkhead.

Mark and Happy plummeted toward Earth at nearly 100 miles an hour. They both had on night vision goggles and infrared lights were blinking from their helmets, allowing them to keep track of one another. The freefall lasted less than two minutes but gave the impression of being much longer in the dark of night.

Their altimeters were set to deploy the chutes at a predetermined distance, as was normal for HALO operations, especially one this dangerous. With the landing zone being on a snow-capped mountain-top, the chutes were set to deploy at 9,000 feet to give them time to stabilize and slow down before reaching the designated coordinates.

Mark felt his parachute deploy, grab the air around him and jerk him upward with whiplash force. Once the canopy fully deployed, he reached up and grabbed the steering toggles. Now in full control of his fall, he attempted to contact Happy. "Hit Man 2, this is Hit Man, do you read me?"

After several attempts Happy finally replied. "I hear you, buddy, I'm about to the target location."

"I must be right on top of you. I can't see your IR light. I'm moving to the east so we don't tangle."

"Roger that."

Happy hit hard and rolled down the mountain in the snow, getting tangled in the strings of his chute before a large rock outcropping stopped him hard, stripping the wind from his lungs. Mark, seeing the ground coming at him, pulled down on the toggles and walked to a soft, textbook landing. Out of nowhere, a gust of wind took him by surprise and knocked him down, re-opening the cells of the parachute before he could unbuckle and get out of it. It dragged him a short distance before he could cut loose and pull in the chute. He checked to make sure he had his gear before calling for Happy.

"I'm wrapped up in the whole damn chute and can barely move," Happy replied.

Mark followed Happy's trail in the snow to get him out of the mess he was in.

The wind blew snow around the men, making the job even more difficult as Mark cut the lines away with his KA-BAR fighting knife.

"We need to dig in until first light," Mark told Happy once he freed him.

They moved to cover on the west side of the mountain where the wind blew calmer. They located a group of rocks and began digging a hole in the snow with entrenching tools. Once done, they had shelter from the elements until it was time to move out.

Mark took first watch after they called in a radio check to the command center and covered the front of the snow cave with their white packs. They left enough uncovered to allow fresh air to circulate.

The next morning before daylight, Happy cooked breakfast meals ready-to-eat in the flameless ration heaters that came with each meal. They had broken the MREs down to the essentials of main courses so they could pack more crucial gear. It wasn't lavish, but it was enough.

The sound of crinkling wrappers woke Mark. "Awe shucks, sweetheart, it's been awhile since anyone brought me breakfast in bed."

"It won't happen again, buddy," Happy replied with a crooked smile.

"Did you looked outside yet?"

"It's not the tropical paradise I had requested, but we're going to have blue skies once the sun comes up. You better break out your sunglasses."

"Roger that."

Mark and Happy ate their field rations of cheese and vegetable omelets. The meals are designed to provide high-calorie content so the operators can maintain rigorous activity for longer periods. The taste wasn't the best, but had improved since the original infantry, "Iron Rations" of World War I.

"We better hit the trail," Happy told Mark once he finished eating.

"Hey, I can't find my TP, please tell me you brought some."

"Sorry, bro, I'm fresh out, it looks like you'll have to do what the locals do and *hand it*."

"Not going to happen! I'll sacrifice my shorts before I resort to Afghan ways," Mark told him.

Mark and Happy had had heard the stories before they witnessed personally, Afghan fighters dropping their trousers, emptying their bowls and wiping their ass with their left hand.

They packed their gear by the light of LED headlamps and left their mountain sanctuary with only weapons and tactical vests to scout the area, before heading down the slopes.

The wind had died down overnight, leaving a cool calmness around them.

The sunlight exploded in brilliance, blinding them as it bounced off the snow and ice. They let their eyes adjust to the light of the cool morning before scouting their flanks. The mountain dominated the landscape, towering above the surrounding peaks like a king on an iron throne, looking down upon his minions.

Mark grabbed his throat mic. "Looks like we're alone up here, bro."

"I agree," Happy responded as they made their way back to their gear.

Mark stood overwatch while Happy applied his cold weather gear and donned his skis. Once he was ready, Mark did the same.

"Are you kidding me?" Happy whispered.

"What?" Mark said while trying to hide a smile.

"Is that your snowboard?"

"Do you know how long it's been since I've carved in powder with Eddie?" Mark asked as he showed the bottom of the board to Happy. The long-haired, zombie-looking man ran the full length of the plank.

"You named your snowboard?"

"It's an Andrew Crawford pro-series, limited edition, and Andy rides with this same Rossignol board. I call mine Eddie because of the Iron Maiden mascot on the bottom."

Happy stood shaking his head before getting on the radio to let command know they were on the move.

"Alright," Mark said as he finished cinching down his bindings, "I'm ready."

# Chapter Twenty-Four
## Tactical Operations Center (TOC)
## Camp Leatherneck
## Sunday, October 12<sup>th</sup>, 0714 Hours

"How are our boys doing this fine morning?" Col. James asked as he walked in the command center, a large stainless-steel mug in hand.

"Both teams made the jump successfully and have started to their first objectives," Howard Spencer spoke up. Being a new addition to the task force, he wanted to make a good impression.

"Very good. Thank you, Mr. Spencer."

Howard smiled, but it quickly vanished when he heard a low "kiss ass" from the corner of the room. Snickers and muffled laughs followed. Spencer had a sharp, analytical mind rivaling or surpassing those on the task force, but some took his intelligence for arrogance.

Two large flat-screen monitors showed the teams making their way down the mountains. The view from the drones came in clear enough to see for miles around.

Gusts of wind kept pushing the tiny aircraft off course, but the pilots were quick to recover.

"Zoom in on Bravo Team," James said.

"It's as close as we can get while they're on the move, sir, especially with the incoming weather," said a young Marine corporal.

"What the hell is that?" the colonel asked as he pointed and squinted at the screen.

"It looks like one of them is riding a snowboard, sir," said another Marine, trying to hide a smirk.

"Damn you, Mitchell!" he roared.

The others in the room knew better than to say anything, but there were lots of smiles. The operators on the task force were always playing pranks on one another, taking any opportunity to have a good time, but Mark Mitchell walked the line no matter the situation.

Nate burst through the door to Memphis' office. "We have a problem, boss."

"I told you to knock before you enter my hooch, boy!"

"This can't wait. We have actionable intelligence." Nate handed him a sheet of paper.

Memphis scanned it. "Who do we have in this AO?"

"Snake and Jigsaw are the closest."

"Tell them to intercept both teams and make it look like locals did the deed. I don't want this to blow back on us."

"Roger that, sir."

Nate left the room muttering something about Mitchell as he made his way to the communications center used by the group. He told the men in the room to leave, closed the door behind them and got on the radio.

"Ratchet, this is Spindle, over," he said across the secured network.

"This is Ratchet," said a deep voice moments later.

"There's movement in your AO. We need you to intercept and destroy. How copy, over."

"Roger that, Spindle. Do you have a location and number of targets?"

"Prepare to receive target coordinates and pertinent info on your PDA. Spindle out."

Nate moved over to a computer, sent the team in the field the two separate grids and told them to use local weapons to accomplish their mission. He gave them the information they currently had on the two teams moving into the valley by sending a burst transmission to the nearest satellite above them. The rugged tablet would receive the data in a matter of seconds. Hacking into the satellites was illegal, but with the amount of encryption they used, no one could track them.

The operators were a few hours away from the first place on the list, Despite the inclement weather, they moved out immediately with a group of local assets and goat herders.

Minutes later, Snake joined Jigsaw and the rest of the men.

"I've received the info and inputted the first set of coordinates into the GPS. Are we ready?"

"Roger that," Jigsaw replied. "It's go time!"

# Chapter Twenty-Five
### High above the Target Valley
### Sunday, October 12<sup>th</sup>, 0937 Hours

Hans and Günther were making their way down the slopes of the mountain on the opposite side of the massive valley from Bravo, as the sun crested the horizon of the razorback ridges to the east. It was slow going with so much gear on as they carved wide swathes in the snow. Descending grew treacherous in some spots. They kept close to the rocks to try and hide their tracks. Even being so high up in elevation, the marks could be seen from below with the right optics. They stopped frequently to check their GPS location and scan the area with binoculars. The vast expanse and stark and stunning scenery of the snow-clad peaks reminded them of the Bavarian Alps, back home in Germany.

"It looks like this nice day is going to slip away soon," Günther remarked when they stopped again. He pointed at gathering dark clouds in the distance.

"We need to get off this mountain as quickly as we can and get to the lower tree line," Hans agreed.

They were making good time as they neared their first objective. They would be swapping out their skis for snowshoes in no time.

Happy stopped above a large rock outcropping and looked back to see where Mark was when powder from the snowboard sprayed him as he turned around.

"What the hell are you doing?" Happy said, annoyed, wiping the snow from his parka, facemask and goggles.

"I'm just having some fun, buddy," Mark chuckled.

"We're close to our first drop point," Happy told him. "We need to swap to our snowshoes."

"Roger that."

They dropped their packs and put their shoes on before putting the skis and snowboard away. They could see the change in the weather and knew they had a limited amount of time before it reached them. The forecasted warm front moving in from the east looked like it would collide with a cold front coming in from the north. The storm could cause numerous issues, but the mission was a priority.

Using their GPS, they navigated the mountain to set up a remote camera in the first assigned position. Unlike drones, the real-time panoramic cameras would monitor the area 24/7 in all weather conditions and could free up men on the ground to accomplish other vital missions.

They set up the camera in an overhang in the rocks cluttering the pass at this elevation. A tiny solar panel would power the camera's rechargeable lithium battery. If positioned correctly, it would rotate and track the sun any time of year but still be hidden enough to not be easily seen. The pneumatic gun they'd brought easily sank the tiny bolts into the granite littering the mountainside to keep the electronics secure even in high winds.

"Did I ever tell you about the time my spotter and I lay in the jungle of Nigeria under triple canopy, in the rain and cold for three days straight to take a shot on a self-proclaimed general of the rebel forces?" Happy piped up as they worked.

"I don't believe you have," Mark said, humoring his partner.

"It was some of the most miserable time I've ever spent in the field and the guy didn't even show. Now, this is the best part, are you ready?"

Mark nodded.

"Because on his way to the rendezvous, his driver hit a cow and rolled their Jeep down a steep embankment, killing them both."

"Hold your thought," Mark said, "I may have something."

Happy continued working and linked the camera to the nearest orbiting satellite using his laptop and called the TOC to make sure they had access to it before he and Mark moved on. "Iron Hide, Iron Hide, this is Hit Man 2, how copy, over."

"Hit Man 2, this is Iron Hide, go ahead with your traffic."

Roger that," Happy replied. "We have a positive link to the first eye on the mountain. How is it on your end?"

"Hit Man 2, we are five-by-five. You can proceed to the next location."

"Roger that. Hit Man 2, out."

Mark had been providing overwatch on Happy's position and noticed some movement on the valley floor. "Iron Hide, this is Hit Man."

"Uh...go ahead Hit Man."

"Iron Hide, what assets do we currently have above our AO?"

"Satellite only. We had to turn the drones around because of the approaching weather front from the north. The wind was too strong to maintain the flight pattern."

Mark provided coordinates to the movement below. Whatever he saw down there was too far away for him to clearly make out and was moving to contact with Charlie Team, posing a huge concern for the mission.

The storm fronts continued to move in fast as Bravo made their way down in elevation. A light granular snow began to fall. They set up two out of three cameras before their comms dissolved to static. The TOC had previously reported that the satellite images were no good due to the clouds blowing over the area. The last camera had been set and linked up, but Happy wasn't able to confirm it was completely operational before he and Mark moved on.

"What's down there?" Günther asked as he put his fist up and stopped near a large, snow covered boulder.

Hans looked through his semi-foggy binoculars. "I can't tell. It might be people or some goats. Are you still not able to reach the TOC?"

"I heard static and broken voices earlier, but now it's all static. I've been in worse weather than this and still had comms. This is very strange."

"Keep trying," Hans told him. "We need to continue moving and reach the lower tree line before dark."

Bravo Team made good time as they descended the mountain. But with the snowstorm and impending night, they knew that going much farther would put them in danger and the operation at risk. Communications were still down, so they found a good place to spend the night and hoped comms would be back up by morning.

"What do you imagine you saw down in the valley this afternoon?" Happy asked as they huddled between the boulders they were using for shelter.

"It may have been goat herders or a nomadic tribe on the move. Whatever it was, I'm sure they're hunkered down for the night, as well. We should reach them in the morning and know for sure."

"If this weather lets up, we might be able to see them."

"Roger that. I'll take first watch, you try and get some sleep."

The wind howled and hissed through the rocks and hard-packed snow outside their little hole in the mountainside.

Neither of them slept much and morning came too fast.

"Is that what I think it is?" Happy asked Mark, then hit him on the arm to wake him.

"What?" Mark said, rubbing the sleep out of his eyes.

"There it is again," Happy said.

They sat up, removed their ponchos and liners, pushed accumulated snow out of the way and listened intently in the wind.

"Yep," Mark said. "Gunfire!"

# Chapter Twenty-Six
### Previously:
### The Valley
### Monday, October 13th, 0724 Hours

"I need you and your men to push the two targets down and to our right flank so we can eliminate them," Snake told the leader of the group of fighters with which they were working.

The large man's eyes were dark and sinister, showing his ruthlessness. He spoke fiercely in Dari to his men and they acted quickly. His face contorted, showing thought being processed on a massive scale as he reached up and pulled on his long, black beard. He pulled back the charging handle on his AK-47 and peered into the chamber to make sure he had a round in it before walking briskly up the side of the mountain, behind his heavily armed, 10 man team.

"Do you think we paid them enough?" Jigsaw asked.

"I do. Besides, they're afraid of the giant in charge. They'd die fighting rather than face him."

Snake and Jigsaw moved south along the bottom of the ridge. The fighters they brought with them would move Charlie Team right into their ambush. With the storm still raging and the low cloud cover, there was no way help would arrive to assist them. And with the active ground-wave jamming upsetting communications in the valley for miles, there would be no hope of calling out. Jigsaw's homemade disrupter sent out a barrage signal stopping each frequency it picked up.

"Hey Snake, any idea why we're taking out four members of the anti-terrorism task force?" Jigsaw asked as they made their way through the valley and accumulating snow.

"Ours is not to question. There must be an extremely good reason, but it's not our concern. We have a job to do and will do it no matter what."

"I know, bro, but these guys are technically the good guys, right?"

"Technically or not, we follow the orders given to us and accomplish the mission by any means necessary."

"All right, let's get this done and head to the next grid coordinates."

It was slow going, but the popping sound of gunfire was an indication the fighters had located the team, moving them toward Snake and Jigsaw. The initial sounds were obviously from a smaller caliber round, like from an M4, but the louder, distinct sound of an AK-47 on full auto could not be mistaken.

"Let's set up here," Snake told his teammate as they reached a cluster of boulders next to a group of trees. The ridge came naturally toward their position on one side and a sheer cliff face with a 100-foot drop spanned the other. It turned into a natural kill zone.

The men dropped their packs and opened the bipods on their Dragonuv sniper rifles chambered in 7.62x54mm. The semiautomatic, gas-operated rifle has a short-stroke, gas-piston system, similar to the AK-47, but with a larger case and longer barrel, it's accurate at much longer distances.

They scanned the area above them and waited for the inevitable arrival of the first of the two teams they'd been sent to kill.

# Chapter Twenty-Seven
### In Contact
### Monday, October 13th, 1016 Hours

"Can you see anything?" Mark asked Happy, who peered through his binoculars.

"There's a sizable force shooting at a smaller one falling back toward the cliff to the south."

"Could it be Charlie Team over there? Are the comms still down?"

"I can't get anything but static."

"All right, let's move closer and find out who's shooting at who."

Mark and Happy continued down the mountain, taking their snowshoes off once they reached the snow line. The firefight on the opposite side of the valley continued sporadically over the next hour as they descended. Along with machine-gun mixed in with other small arms fire, they heard explosions from grenades and possibly RPGs. Happy checked the range to the adjacent side whenever they stopped. They would be in range of targets in no time.

"Look there," Happy said.

"It looks like the force on the run was flanked and is now caught in a cross fire."

"Mark," Happy dropped his binoculars on his chest. "It's Charlie Team in the middle!"

A red starburst flare erupted above the trees. The shear brilliance was a real eye catcher even with the low-lying clouds. It was an indication of a friendly force in trouble and requesting assistance. With no way to call for close air support, it was up to Bravo Team. The long distance to the targets and the weather conditions would make it difficult, but they had to try.

"Ahh!" Hans yelled, cursing in German as another bullet from the fast-approaching enemy force tore through soft tissue on his right upper thigh. He turned, acquired a target and sent a burst of full auto downrange at the man from his silenced HK G28 modular rifle chambered in 7.62x51mm. The hot lead of the large bullets hit the attacker and the tree next to him, sending splinters and blood into the air. Hans spun and shot at another target nearby. He fired three rounds from his rifle at the aggressor, followed by a *click*. Without missing a beat, Hans dropped his rifle so it hung free in front of him, grabbed his Glock .45 from its holster on his leg and sent a volley of bullets downrange.

Both men from Charlie Team had been shot multiple times, but with body armor covering most of their vital organs their wounds were not yet critical. The sustained firefight not only took its toll on them physically but had rapidly depleted their ammo. The trees and smooth boulders blanketing the ridge made it hard to see the insurgents until their muzzle flashes gave them away like the flint-wheel of a Zippo sparking in the distance.

"We need to make a decision," Günther said, as he fired a few rounds through the fog at movement to his right.

"I know. I'm down to only a few magazines for each weapon and one grenade," Hans replied.

Another PKM burst exploded toward the men, disintegrating the rocks around them. They ducked to avoid getting hit again by the granite dust and shrapnel.

"How many men are out there?"

"I don't know, but we can't keep this up for much longer."

"I know — I'm going to push left. Cover me."

They decided to make a stand near a cluster of trees below them. They would use them as cover and lure the enemy in, trying to kill enough of them so they could either turn the tide, or get away. They still hadn't broken out their sniper rifle, the German DSR-1 chambered in .338 Lapua Magnum that Günther had in his pack. So far they hadn't needed the long-range weapon, but it might become their last resort. They still heard only static from the radio, preventing them from calling for help, and the mist continued to obscure their vision. Another RPG round fired at them. It exploded at the base of a tree in front of Hans. The blast threw him into Günther and both men tumbled farther down the hill, causing them to lose their main radio and more of their gear. They came to rest below the layer of fog covering most of the ridge. They checked their weapons, ammo and gear, before taking fire from a new direction — from below.

They positioned themselves back to back with Hans pointing his rifle up toward the initial attackers. They scanned both directions with their scopes and started shooting.

"Günther, I will..." Hans started to say as he changed magazines, but stopped as he was sprayed with a warm, red mist from behind.

"Any word from our team?" Memphis asked Nate as he walked into the comm. room trailed by someone Nate hadn't seen before.

"Nothing yet, boss. They must still be in contact and jamming radio frequencies. The net is going crazy about two teams in possible trouble who won't respond to radio calls."

"Keep me apprised of the situation."

"Will do," Nate told him.

"I want you to get over to the operations center and see if there's anything we don't already know. And, H, try not to attract any unnecessary attention. Your orders for the task force should arrive soon, so try and blend in for now. If you're questioned, tell them you were able to get on an earlier flight. Headquarters told me you already have your mission parameters. I don't like not knowing, but as usual, I trust there's a good reason."

A grunt and a shake of the head was enough for Memphis. This operator, recently sent to him from headquarters in Maryland, had a reputation for only talking when it was pertinent, and was apparently as deadly as a black widow. Memphis didn't relish the idea of finding out first-hand. The reputation preceding this operator was enough for him.

Personnel from Executive Security who weren't out on missions worked feverishly to get rid of any evidence of current and past missions. Shredders were making quick work of paper documents and computer techs were busy with the electronic ones per Dennis Ryland's orders. Memphis knew it was only a matter of time before they were investigated on allegations of wrong-doing. Even though he was simply following orders from higher than his pay grade, he truly believed the work he and his men were doing, was in the best interest of the country he loved and for which he bled . Whatever the endgame was, he wasn't privy. Even though he knew there should be a damn good reason for what they did, he felt like he needed to cover his own ass.

# Chapter Twenty-Eight
## In Contact +
### Monday, October 13th, 1156 Hours

The bullet that hit Günther tore through his neck right below his right ear. The arterial spray from his jugular pumped out at a fast rate, covering the surrounding rocks and vegetation. Hans assessed the man from behind the rocks. Even if a medic had been nearby, he still would've bled out.

Hans and his teammate's body were now somewhat hidden between two large boulders, but he was still a sitting duck. The large German stripped the remaining ordnance off his friend's body and began fighting again. He alternated shooting between the two attacking forces until he saw both positions were taking fire from somewhere else. He welcomed the reprieve but stayed vigilant and shot at what he could identify as the forces above him continued to close in.

As Mark moved into position behind the rifle, he remembered the last time he had competed at Camp Perry. He took second in the nationals behind his long-time rival, James Perkins. The wind blew hard then, as well. It wasn't forecasted but had picked up in intensity off Lake Erie as the day progressed. Mark had lost by one point. It had been a constant struggle to beat the man. He had been interviewed for the Marine Corps Times afterward by a corporal hailing from South Carolina. She was a young, vibrant and smart as a whip too.

The question that stuck with Mark the most had been, "Staff Sergeant, you've been to combat and have confirmed kills as a sniper. What do you feel after you pull the trigger to kill a man, vs. shooting at paper?"

"Well, Corporal," he'd told her. "I feel exactly the same whenever I pull the trigger on my rifle, no matter the target.

"Which is?"

He couldn't resist. "Right as the crisp trigger breaks and surprises me, as it should, I feel... a slight recoil in my shoulder."

Mark and Happy were rushed into setting up, but they knew they had to help. Mark didn't want to silhouette himself, wanted to avoid crest lines, but he needed to start engaging the enemy. Minutes later, Bravo Team was ready and firing.

Being so far away, the travel time of each round sent downrange continued to miss the targets. Mark had a difficult time adjusting for the target's movement with so much wind in the mix, even with the heavy bullet of his .50 cal. He and Happy came up with a plan they hoped would work.

"You go first," Mark told Happy.

When they were set, Mark nudged Happy's boot to let him know he was ready. Happy fired first and Mark a few seconds later. It worked — the first enemy combatant fell to the ground as Mark's bullet found its home. They continued to fire at the largest group of insurgents after slowing the smaller one down with an especially evident hit.

Mark kept shooting as Happy stopped to reload and heard the radio come to life. "Hit Man, this is Iron Hide, do you copy?"

Happy reached for the handset. "Iron Hide, this is Hit Man 2, I read you loud and clear. We need air support forthwith to..."

Mark continued to engage the threat on the other side of the valley when he saw a helmet roll down the slope in front of him. He looked back and saw Happy lying face down on a flat rock, blood pooling under him. Bullets continued to ricochet off the rocks near them, sending shrapnel and rock chips everywhere. Mark stayed on his rifle and sent more microchip implants downrange so the insurgents could talk to Allah easier.

"All right buddy, I'm coming," Mark told Happy once he couldn't find any more active targets to engage. His friend, his comrade in arms wasn't moving. Blood flowed like a river. He saw the radio and picked up the handset. "Iron Hide, Iron Hide, this is Hit Man... Answer me, *damn you.*"

"Hit Man, this is Iron Hide."

"Troops in contact!" Mark yelled. "I'm requesting close air support and a medevac. Hit Man 2 is KIA and Charlie Team is under heavy enemy fire, how copy, over."

"Hit Man, I need a grid." It was the colonel.

# Chapter Twenty-Nine
### Camp Leatherneck
### Task Force Briefing Room
### Three Days Later

"That was a close one," Howard Spencer told Mark. "I still can't believe you gave Happy a direct blood transfusion right there in the field with people shooting at you."

"I did what I had to. The shooting had stopped and the colonel told me help was coming. Happy was in hypovolemic shock. I stabilized him, stopped the bleeding and began the transfer like I had been trained to do. I knew the cold would aid the process and help preserve him longer if I could revive him."

"I'm still in awe. You helped him while calling in the enemy's position. You know you're a hero right?"

"Luckily the bullet only grazed Happy's skull and I had been able to help him. I was only doing my job."

"When the Delta Force platoon finally reached you, they thought both of you were dead."

"I know, I heard all about it."

Men were filtering into the conference room for the morning briefing. Conversation was abundant, as usual, and the smell of coffee filled the air. Mark stood near the door finishing his conversation with Howard Spencer when something caught his attention in his right peripheral. Someone lunged at him, throwing a fist, which he blocked and assumed a counter-attack stance.

"Mitchell, meet Hephzibah Romach," the colonel said as he strolled in the room behind her. "She'll be Happy's replacement while he's recovering from his wounds."

Her long black hair was pulled up tight in a bun but Mark could easily tell how beautiful she was. She had a petite frame, but even through her BDUs he could see it was all muscle. And those eyes! They were as blue as the Mediterranean Sea, yet as icy as the Arctic Ocean.

"It's very nice to meet you Mark, or do you prefer Mitchell?" she said.

Stunned and caught off guard, Mark regained his composure and mustered, "What the hell, lady?"

"I read your jacket and saw you're proficient in Krav Maga and I wanted to see for myself. You're pretty quick. I would like to spar with you some time. That is, if you presume you can handle me."

"Colonel, I don't need another spotter. I can work fine on my own until Happy gets better. I only kept him around for his humor anyway. Other than that the guy's pretty much useless," Mark said, which the colonel ignored. The truth was that Happy was indispens-able. They were like brothers. Mark was entrusted with Happy's well-being, and he with Mark's.

Cat-calls and whistles came from the other oper-ators in the room. "Looks like you've been called out Mitchell. Let me know if you want *me* to tame the wild-cat for you," offered Hans Richter from Charlie Team.

"In your dreams," Hephzibah snapped back.

"You don't know what you're missing, Fräulein."

"OK," boomed the colonel. "Sit down and listen up. Men, this is Hephzibah Romach. She's going to be taking Happy's place on Bravo Team until he recovers from his wounds. She's on loan to us, but I want each of you to treat her with the respect you would give to any team member. She's a former Mossad intelligence officer and is proficient in hand-to-hand combat, small arms and counter-insurgency. She is also an accom-plished IDF sniper and will be invaluable in the days and weeks to come. Mr. Spencer, if you please."

"All right," Spencer started, then cleared his throat. "With the recent events, we have a new game plan. The attack on Bravo and Charlie Teams is still under investigation. However, the American who was found with the insurgents has been discovered to have previously worked for Executive Security."

The room exploded with questions and was silenced by the colonel.

"A spokesperson for the company said the man had gone off the reservation some time ago, which has been confirmed by their man in charge in country, Frank Holliday, or Memphis, as some of you know him," Spencer continued.

"And, what? We're gonna believe them?" Valentine spoke up.

"We have no reason not to take them at their word at this point," Col. James retorted.

"Do we have any intel from the last OP we were on?" Mark asked, changing the subject.

"So far, it's extremely quiet in the region. More weather fronts have moved in and made it hard to see much," Spencer told him. "Until we get something concrete to go off of, the joint mission with the Afghan Army has been put on hold."

"It sounds like you're saying Happy was shot and Günther died for nothing!" Hans protested.

"The Delta operators who came to your assistance found seven dead enemy combatants and the one American," Spencer reassured him. "You guys gave them hell, and after being shot four times yourself, you should still be at the aid station or back in Germany."

Hans started spouting off in German about flesh wounds. Col. James intervened.

"In the meantime, we're all going to get some range time in," the colonel said. "Most of you have been on active missions as of late, but others have not. We also need to evaluate the new people."

"I would imagine our reputations and service records would tell you everything you need to know," chimed in the new member of Charlie Team, Dieter Gehring. Dieter had served with Hans and Günther in the KSK years before and was known for being confrontational, but also showed pragmatic and icy professionalism.

"I say you put your money where your mouth is, big boy," Hephzibah challenged.

"You're on, sweetheart," Dieter told her with a smile and a wink.

"All right people, we have the range from 1500 to 2200 hours today. Col. James said. "Get your weapons and gear ready and don't be late."

"2200?" A voice from the back complained.

"Yes, ladies, there will be a day and night shoot, so pack accordingly. Mitchell, you and Romach come and see me before you gear up. I volunteered you two to assist in the training of Afghan soldiers at an Army outpost tomorrow so you can get used to how each other works. I want to brief you before this evolution."

The operators slowly moved out of the room, some still complaining. Mark, being at the back of the crowd, was one of the last to leave. He saw his new teammate's gaze linger on him.

They exchanged curious glances before she turned and walked out.

# Chapter Thirty
## Baltimore, Maryland
## Top Floor of the Executive
## Security Building
## Monday, October 13th, 1924 Hours

"What the hell happened, Dennis?" Tom demanded. "That's three fuckups in less than a week!"

"Memphis made the call, and in his defense sir, I believe it was the right one at the time. He saw an opportunity to finish what the Russian started, but there's no way he could anticipate all the factors involved. The men he sent happened to be some of the best we've ever had the pleasure to serve with."

"I know, I served with Scott personally and was aware of what he was capable of. Jigsaw he was called, from his knife fights for money. He always came back to base with new cuts on his body. He nearly lost an eye in Panama and really pissed off the commander we served under. Regardless, we're under the microscope in that region now. I want the Emerald Operation in

Afghanistan temporarily shut down and Memphis to be relieved of his command early. We have to make examples and be accountable for our people. "

"The locals won't be happy."

"I don't give a damn, Dennis. They don't run the show. We do. Now make it happen!"

"Consider it done, boss."

"Good. Now, is the new operative in place?"

"She arrived in country two days ago and is fitting in nicely."

"Fantastic. I want an update once a day. Dennis, we need to do better."

"Will do, sir."

Dennis left the room and walked into Katarina's office at the end of the hall. She was on the phone as he shut the door behind him, locked it and rolled down the blinds.

She hung up as he approached her desk. "What do you suppose you're doing?" she questioned Dennis as she stood up.

"I believe we need to talk, little lady. Certain issues have gotten out of hand and someone needs to answer for the mistakes."

"Well, maybe you should punish the person responsible then," she stated unequivocally.

"Oh, I plan to," Dennis told her as he walked around to her side of the desk.

She picked up the phone and he grabbed it, slamming the receiver back down.

"What do you think you're doing?" he demanded.

"I was going to call for security."

"You don't need to."

"Why not?" she asked, raising her eyebrows.

"Because, I'm all you need."

Dennis grabbed Katarina and kissed her hard as she tried to pull away. She slapped him across the face, leaving a mark. He turned her around, pulled up her skirt and smacked her right cheek, leaving a hand mark of his own. She let out a squeal.

"Do I have the right person? Do you need to be punished?"

"Yes, please," she said, looking back and smiling.

Dennis continued to spank and disrobe Katarina as he bent her over the desk. He knew it wouldn't last forever between them, but he intended to enjoy himself while he could. Memphis would be back in short order and play-time would end. Dennis felt no guilt about it. After all, Frank had ruined his marriage years ago. Dennis was getting a little payback and having fun doing it. Katarina wasn't privy to any of it and didn't need to find out, as far as he was concerned.

"All's fair in love and war," Dennis grunted.

# Chapter Thirty-One
## Camp Leatherneck Shooting Range
### Thursday, October 16th, 1843 Hours

The 40-foot sand berms surrounding the make-shift shooting range on the outskirts of the base allowed for base personnel to safely shoot small arms, from handguns to machineguns. The Navy Seabees had done a great job in the construction of the base and additions like this one.

For the last part of the afternoon, the task force operators ran shooting drills on failure to fire, magazine changes and transition from primary to secondary weapons in each position. Instructors covered weak-hand shooting, as well as firing while recovering a teammate. All personnel were proficient in the different types of execution, but regular training kept them sharp. In one evolution, shooting at multiple targets while moving to cover, one of the Brits had a malfunction with his handgun and pulled his fighting knife to take out his last target. Even though they would've done it also, laughter erupted from some of the men behind the firing line.

The range safety officer called another cease-fire, this time to transition from daytime shooting to nighttime. The sun had gone down and the light on the horizon turned to twilight. After holstering their handguns and putting the rifles in Condition 4 — weapon on safe, bolt home on an empty chamber with no magazine inserted — the shooters mustered back at one of the several metal Conex boxes behind the firing line to retrieve more ammo.

"Listen up, people," Col. James shouted. "The chow truck will be here shortly, so stop jaw jacking and change out your targets and optics for the next evolution. We will begin once it's dark enough."

Mark approached Col. James and asked to talk to him alone.

"What is it, Mitchell?"

"Colonel, I've been doing some digging on my own and I believe we're looking in the wrong places. The attacks, not only on coalition personnel, but on our joint anti-terrorism task force, have to be coming from higher up in the food chain."

"We have our own investigators, Mitchell, and you need to steer clear of this. Give me the information you have and *I* will pass it on. After this, I want you to stay out of it. Am I clear?"

"Crystal clear, sir. Now, all evidence points to Executive Security and its operators, right? The crates Happy and I saw in the Dungeon were the same ones we've seen transported from the mountains to Pakistan."

"What's your point, Mitchell?"

"It all appears to be a little too convenient."

"How do you mean?"

"The men from Executive Security happen to be well-trained former military personnel and wouldn't make a mistake like this. I imagine there's someone higher up framing them to take the spotlight off the real culprits."

"Ludicrous, Mitchell! It's nothing more than a few men, like the one you shot, trying to set themselves up for retirement."

"Maybe, but can we at least take this possibility up the chain of command and see what they believe?"

"Not no, but hell no! You will stand down and forget this nonsense! Now get out there and get ready for the night shoot."

Mark watched as the colonel walked away. Something didn't add up and he had to find out what was really going on, for Happy, Günther and the other men who had been killed or hurt because of this. In the meantime, some more trigger time to take out his aggression always helped. The aroma of lingering burnt gunpowder in the air smelled like an aphrodisiac. It was a perfect ending to the evening.

"Is everything OK?" Hephzibah asked as she approached Mark.

"It will be soon enough."

# Chapter Thirty-Two
## Combat Outpost 'Sidewinder' (COP)
### Kunar Province
### Friday, October 17th, 1428 Hours

"Incoming!" several soldiers screamed as mortar rounds exploded inside the base leaving small craters in their wake and sending dust plumes skyward. The men could be heard even over the sound of the helicopters engines and massive rotor wash on the loose red dirt.

Two RPG rounds snaked past the CH-47's front rotor as it landed on the raised pad of the COP inside the Hesco bag wall skirting the tiny outpost. The large bags filled with dirt and rocks shield friendly troops from incoming bullets and grenades.

"You Americans sure know how to show a girl a good time," said Hephzibah while she changed magazines in her rifle. She closed the bolt, ramming a fresh, live round into the already searing chamber, then assessed and engaged again. "I thought this was just going to be a training mission and familiarization?"

"Yeah, well, nobody's perfect. What are you complaining about? At least you were able to get out of the house," Mark replied as he sent another volley of bullets toward the front gate where a couple insurgents attempted to get through.

Mortar rounds were striking the east section of the perimeter and the soldiers were taking a beating. A few Afghan National Army Soldiers abandoned their posts and fled to ground in the bunkers that had been designed for noncombat personnel.

The helo lifted off with soldiers aboard. They had been training the ANA on the speck of land for counter-insurgency along the border. Mark and Hephzibah were there to assist. Their aircraft had dusted off without them.

Small arms and machine-gun fire were raining down on the outpost from an elevated position across the valley. RPG rounds were being fired at the west wall and towers. The enemy must've been unaware that no one was there. Besides a few stragglers, most of the troops from the COP had gone into the bunkers like they had been told to do when they had incoming. Explosions were rocking inside the perimeter and Mark could see grenades rolling in toward the tiny gym the soldiers had set up.

"It's a diversion," Mark told his teammate. "They've made it inside."

The two members of Bravo Team moved to contact on the south end of the compound. An insurgent walked around the corner of the sandbag and plywood structure. Mark saw the barrel of the AK before he saw the man, clad in black from head to toe. They both raised their rifles at the same time but before Mark pulled the trigger, shots rang out from the kitchen area of the chow hall. One of the Army cooks hadn't made it to the bunker when mortar rounds began pounding the area.

"Nice shooting!" Mark said to the soldier who stood there shaking.

"Thanks," he murmured.

"Were you the only one in there?" Hephzibah asked.

"Huh...uh, yeah it was only me. The others left as soon as the mortars started falling."

"Listen," Mark began. "I want you to go down into the bunker and get whoever's down there. Tell them we need their help with the last of the insurgents."

"OK, I'll go get them."

More shooting caught Mark's attention. He and Hephzibah moved toward the sound of a duel between a couple of AKs and M4s.

An enemy soldier ran at them firing from the hip and spraying bullets, none of which came anywhere close to them. The insurgent stopped firing after he emptied his magazine. He dropped to his knees and fumbled with the rifle.

Hephzibah ran toward the enemy combatant who tried desperately to insert a loaded magazine into his ancient Russian AK-47. She dropped her rifle onto the ground and the weapon kicked up dust as it landed in the loose soil. He stood and contemplated running but decided he could take the woman coming at him. She ran up the man as if she were scaling a wall. Her petite legs found their way to his neck and wrapped around it like an MMA fighter. Her weight shifted and she took the massive insurgent to the ground with a *thud*, a dirt cloud rising above them. She twisted her body and snapped his neck. Mark walked up behind her, shaking his head.

"Couldn't you have just shot him?" he asked.

"This was much more fun," she said while she dusted herself off.

They heard more shooting from the direction they'd been heading. Mark handed Hephzibah her rifle.

They moved in behind soldiers who were shooting at the 40-foot metal Conex box that contained much of their perishable foods.

"What do you boys have over here?" Mark asked when they were close enough to be heard.

A soldier wheeled around, pointing his rifle toward Bravo Team. Mark grabbed the barrel and pushed it up into the air as a burst of rounds fired off.

"Friendly!" Mark screamed at him.

"Damn! I'm real sorry," drawled a deep Southern voice. You scared the shit out of me!"

An explosion erupted by the Hesco bag wall they were standing near. Seconds later, another explosion detonated.

"There's a couple of the damn haji's holed up in the kitchen's Conex," said a soldier with captain's bars on his collars. "They keep throwing grenades out."

Soldiers moved in behind them, responding to Mark's request for backup.

"Captain, if we throw some smoke out there, we can maneuver around to the other side and toss a grenade in the front door," Mark suggested.

"Sir, should we attach a small amount of C4 to the wall and take them out? I don't know of any of us stupid enough to open the doors and try to..."

"That's a great idea, make a shape charge and get it on the left side of the box," the captain ordered, cutting him off.

"Captain, my partner and I can get this done so you don't have to damage the container," Mark told him.

"Who the hell are you two?"

"We're DOD contractors flown in this morning to help train your ANA soldiers."

"We have this under control and don't need your help. Stand down. That's an order."

The explosives ordnance technician said he was ready about ten minutes later. White smoke popped near the doors of the container and the man moved with another soldier through the haze. Minutes later they returned and were ready to remote detonate the charge.

"Let me do it," said the captain.

The technician handed the officer the detonator. The explosion knocked a few soldiers off their feet. The charge had been larger than expected. Once the dust settled, the metal container looked as if a tank round had hit it dead center. Shrapnel from the container stuck out of the Hesco bag wall. The remains of the creased and twisted metal box lay smoldering. Chunks of wood took off like wildfire. The troop barracks and chow hall were set ablaze.

Seven insurgents had been killed during the battle, which lasted a little over an hour. One wounded enemy combatant was taken into custody. A medevac had been called for three wounded soldiers and the insurgent. Fixed-wing and rotor aircraft filled the sky above the valley as more air support moved in. Explosions rocked the ridge from where the mortar and small arms rounds had come. Mark and Hephzibah jumped on the medevac chopper headed to Kandahar air base. Once they felt the aircraft lift off and gain altitude, Mark and Hephzibah looked at each other. No one could hear them over the loud noise of the engines and avionics, but they couldn't stop laughing.

# Chapter Thirty-Three
**Camp Leatherneck Recreation Tent**
**The Next Morning**

"Is that all you have?" Hephzibah grunted as she maneuvered again, avoiding a hook punch, while sweeping Mark to the ground with her right leg.

"I've got plenty left!" But Mark was breathing heavily as he posted his right arm on the floor, jumping to his feet and into a fighting stance.

At 0400, with no one else around, it was a perfect time to spar with a partner. Mark didn't want an audience. He'd never been one for the spotlight.

Sweat covered the floor mat. Hephzibah was relentless with her attacks. She threw palm heel strikes followed with elbow strikes in combination with back kicks and spinning heel kicks. She was good, and Mark was enjoying the early morning workout.

"I can tell you're holding back, Mitchell," she told him before she threw a round kick at his knee.

"I don't want to hurt my new partner."

Mark easily blocked her advance, countering with a double-leg takedown maneuver. She landed on the mat hard, knocking the wind out of her. Mark pushed her legs out of the way. She rolled to maneuver back to her feet, but Mark proved too fast and succeeded in getting her in a guillotine choke from the front. Hephzibah threw several punches but Mark didn't relent. She eventually fell unconscious. Mark lay her down on the mat, knowing she would wake shortly.

Much to his surprise, she suddenly came back to life and swept his legs. He hit the floor. She rolled on top of him and went to finish him off with an elbow strike to the face. She stopped short of making contact.

"That was unexpected," Mark told her.

"What, you've never had a woman play opossum before?"

They both lay on the mat, catching their breath. As they rolled toward one another their eyes met. Mark felt her hot breath on his face, her heart beating rapidly as their lips neared.

The front door opened and slammed as someone entered the tent. More lights flicked on as Mark and Hephzibah moved to their feet and grabbed their towels.

Mark offered a handshake to his new teammate. "Thanks for the workout. We'll have to do it again soon."

Hephzibah smiled and shook his hand firmly. "I can't wait until next time."

*That was close*, Mark thought.

More people were entering the tent, so Mark and Hephzibah left to shower and get ready for the day. They were still on standby for the joint mission with the Afghans and they were all on rotation for duty in the TOC.

Before reporting for duty in the afternoon, Mark stopped by the aid station to see Happy, who'd been put in a medically induced coma because of the swelling on his brain. He was lucky to be alive after losing so much blood. He would have been sent to the Kandahar Airfield Medical Treatment Facility, but the doctors didn't want to risk moving him once he arrived on Leatherneck.

Duke stood in Happy's room when Mark arrived, and Schnell walked around the side of the bed her ears perked up once she heard Mark's voice. "How's he doing, brother?"

"The doc says they should be able to bring him out in a day or two. His vitals appear strong and he should recover fully."

"Sounds great," Mark said, petting Schnell. "Have they figured out why he keeps drooling?"

"Apparently he has nerve damage as a result of the wound he received on his face last week," Duke told him.

"Now this makes more sense. He's had a hell of a time smiling and he smiles constantly. I thought it was because of the stitches."

They laughed, a passing nurse shushing them, causing them to laugh even louder.

"I hear you have a new partner?"

"She's only temporary until Happy gets better."

"She?"

"Yep, she's Israeli, and according to her records, one to be reckoned with."

"I bet she is," Duke smiled as they left the building.

"Thanks again for watching Schnell."

"Anytime. She's been a great help keeping the patrons in line. It's actually refreshing having another Marine around."

"I'm glad. I'll stop by later, Duke. I need to go talk to someone."

# Chapter Thirty-Four
## Camp Leatherneck
### Saturday, October 18th, 1537 Hours

He watched from the shadows of the building as the talk became an argument. She turned to leave. He watched her walk away, trying to call after her. She didn't turn around, so he left as well, walking the opposite way. Mark walked after her. Curiosity had the better of him.

Mark followed her past a few buildings but she had disappeared.

"Something I can help you with, Mitchell?"

Mark turned. There stood Hephzibah Romach. "Nope, I don't think so. I was on my way back to my room to retrieve a folder I forgot. I need it for my shift at the TOC."

"You sure you weren't following me?"

"Now why would I follow you?

"Maybe you saw me talking to Memphis?"

"You know Memphis? He's a great guy isn't he?"

"He's my ex and a son of a bitch. Listen, I know you saw us arguing. What I can't understand is why you're following me. You're not keeping tabs on me, are you?"

"I just found it odd that my new partner was talking to a person of interest in an ongoing investigation. I saw you when I was leaving the hospital. I didn't know you two had history. My apologies. It won't happen again."

"I'll see to you later, partner," she said with a wink.

Mark stood there for a moment to process what had happened before going on to the TOC.

"Sir, we have movement by camera 4," a young corporal announced.

"What do we have?" Mark asked as he approached the wall with monitors displaying the real-time images of the mountains.

"I saw a blur of light on this screen, then it was gone."

"Switch to night vision."

"Nothing, sir, it's a black screen."

"Bring up thermal."

"Still nothing, sir."

"I want all cameras turned to thermal. Sergeant, get me Kandahar operations. I want to know if they have any birds in the air in the region."

"Roger that, sir."

"Sir," the corporal said. "We may have a problem."

"Wake Col. James and get him over here now!"

"You want me to wake him, sir?"

"Did I stutter, Corporal? Pick up the phone and call him right now!"

Mark looked at the images on the remaining screens showing people approaching the cameras. The monitors displayed figures until they all went dark.

"This isn't good, is it, sir?" The corporal asked Mark while he picked up the phone next to him.

"Not good at all, and the reason you're waking the colonel."

"Sir, I have a Major Thomas on the line. He says he has a Global Hawk in the area already and he can have a Reaper inbound in 20 minutes," the sergeant said.

"I want the Reaper airborne immediately and I want real-time images from both aircraft brought up on our screens now," Mark instructed, handing him a slip of paper. "Give Thomas this grid first."

"What the hell is going on, Mitchell?" Col. James didn't look happy as he burst through the door.

"Sir, all of our surveillance of the Hindu Kush region has been taken offline."

"Was it destroyed, or is there a glitch?"

"Corporal, bring up the last recorded images," Mark told him.

James and the rest of the men in the room watched the screens and saw them go dark, one by one.

"Do we have any birds in the area?" the colonel asked.

"We're in contact with the Air Force at Kandahar right now," Mark said. "They already had a Global

Hawk in the AO and I've instructed them to send a Reaper there immediately. We should have images soon."

"They're coming through now," the sergeant said.

Col. James looked at Mark. "What the hell is going on up there?"

# Chapter Thirty-Five
**Joint Task Force TOC, Camp
Leatherneck
Saturday, October 18<sup>th</sup>, 2217 Hours**

The image on the screen from the Global Hawk at 50,000 feet showed multiple heat signatures surrounding the area where most of the cameras had been.

"Sir, the Reaper is now over the target area," the sergeant said.

"What do you want to do, sir?" Mark asked Col. James.

"Do we know if they're hostile or friendly?"

"They're there and our cameras have stopped working. I would venture to say they aren't on our side. There's a short list of people who knew we installed them."

"Without confirmation I'm not going to order a strike. They could be friendly forces or civilians, for all we know."

"Sir, I've checked twice," the sergeant spoke up. "We have no friendly forces in the region or anywhere close."

"We need to take those targets out," Mark said.

"Not without confirmation," Col. James said.

"Colonel, they took out the cameras. If we don't act now, we might not have another chance."

"Shut it down."

"Sir?" Mark said.

"All of it — shut it down. Tell Kandahar we don't need them any longer and you men can leave the room."

Mark wanted to argue and could tell some of the Marines did as well, but they complied with the orders. A few minutes later they were turning off the lights and leaving.

Mark had barely settled in his bed with a copy of Stephen King's "Doctor Sleep" when he heard a knock at his door.

"Who is it?" He approached the door with his .45 in hand.

"It's Hephzibah. Can we talk?"

"Give me a minute."

If it had been Happy or nearly anyone else, he would've simply opened the door. This time, he put on a pair of trousers and a Metallica t-shirt.

He lifted the 2-by-4 out of the way and cracked the door. "What's going on? Are you OK?"

"I know it's late, but I wanted to talk about what happened earlier. I wanted to make sure... I mean, if we're going to be teammates, we need to trust each other, right?"

"I completely agree. Please come in. Would you like a beer, or water?"

"A beer would be great," she said, smiling.

Mark opened his mini fridge and grabbed two cold ones before sitting on the edge of his bed. "What's on your mind?"

"I know I've only been with the task force for a few days, but I sense a connection to you. I can't explain it."

"I've enjoyed your company, as well, but I know it's in everyone's best interest if we keep our relationship on a professional level."

"Mark, I agree with you whole-heartedly." Yet her hand made contact with Mark's thigh as she looked around the room, seeing the picture on the table next to the bed. "Who's this little guy? Your son?"

"He's nobody," Mark said, turning the frame over, wanting to avoid that conversation.

"I've seen your file, Mark. I know what happened. It wasn't your fault. You can't keep blaming yourself."

Mark took a swig of his beer and looked away. The guilt felt overwhelming. He knew it would never go away.

"It's OK to be vulnerable. We are soldiers, but we are also human. I lost a child, too. Ariella was my little angel, and losing her crushed me." Hephzibah looked up, her eyes welling with tears.

"Hey, it's all right." Mark took the beer out of her hand and set them both on the floor. He pulled her close. "I didn't know. I'm so sorry."

She buried her face in his chest. He felt the wetness of her tears and the heat of her breath through his thin t-shirt. She choked and spasmed trying to control her emotions.

"I'm sorry, Mark. I don't know what came over me."

"It's fine. I have those feelings too sometimes. Losing a loved one is hard, but losing a child. No one should have to endure such a loss."

She lay down, pulling him behind her. "I didn't come here for this, but could you hold me awhile?"

Mark knew he shouldn't, but he felt no tension. It felt natural in a way he hadn't felt in a long time. "For a while," he whispered into her hair.

She pulled his arm around her and snuggled close. She took a long, deep breath and let out a shuddering sigh. He knew the sensation. She felt safe in his arms. They were as close as lovers but they barely knew each other.

*What the hell are you doing, Mitchell? Damn, she smells good. Is that jasmine? Damn, she feels good! Don't do it, man! Let her fall asleep and don't let this happen again.*

"Mark," she whispered.

Hesitating, Mark finally replied."Yes?"

She rolled over and kissed his cheek. "Thank you."

He felt her breath on his neck as she rolled into him. A hint of mint overpowered the little drink of beer she'd had. "Don't mention it." She looked up at him with her blue eyes and he spoke before he even realized it. "God, you're beautiful."

She kissed him, softly at first. An electric current jolted from his lips to his toes and he pulled her even closer. They kissed hard and deep, coming up for air a couple of times while they found each other's bodies. Her hands moved under his shirt and she raked his chest with her fingernails. "I want you," she said.

He twisted his fingers into her hair, pulling her head back and kissing her neck. She moaned as she leaned her body into his. Hephzibah stood up to undress herself. As each piece of clothing hit the floor, Mark bit his lip harder. Her long, lean body was perfection. Naked, she crawled to him, pausing to unbutton his pants and slide them down. He kicked them off his feet as she pulled his shirt up and over his head.

He pressed against her, hinting the urgency of the situation. She moaned in his ear, biting at his lobe. Unable to restrain himself, he pushed her hips down to meet him. She pulled away, causing him to curse in frustration.

"Do you know what you're doing to me?" he whispered.

"I think I have an idea. Let me put you out of your misery."

Slowly she lowered herself to him. Mark felt intensity unlike anything before. Rolling over to take charge, Mark increased the pace. Hephzibah held her breath as her body shuddered, her moans getting louder. As Mark lost control he felt her tension release as she moaned again. Their hearts pounded against each other and sweat covered them head to toe.

"Adoni shelei," she mustered.

Mark gasped for breath. "Not God, honey. I'm merely a man."

Hephzibah rolled over and looked at him. Her cheeks were as flushed as a red rose and her chest was speckled with ruby-colored dots from her orgasm. She pulled him to her, softly kissing in a line from his chest to his neck and his lips. They drifted off to sleep.

# Chapter Thirty-Six
## Camp Leatherneck
### Sunday, October 19th, 0137 Hours

The earthquake intensified. A siren sounded in the distance. The floor shook, inducing vertigo like an old-fashioned wooden roller-coaster plummeting from its most vertical drop. Mark heard loud hammering as the rickety car threatened to jump the tracks. He was finding it harder to breathe as the car picked up speed when someone grabbed him as if to pull him to safety.

"Wake up, Mark!"

Mark jerked awake in his bed. Hans stood over him.

"What the hell's going on?" Mark asked, looking around the room. Hephzibah was gone.

"The base is under attack! We need to get out there now!"

"How large of a force is attacking?"

"I don't know, but from the sounds of it, *massive*."

Mark dressed quickly, put on his gear and followed Hans. A long, rectangular ceiling light dangled from wires outside his door. Sparks erupted from it as it dangled on the brink of falling. Other lights flickered and surged as the men moved on. Part of the structure had collapsed and bodies were lying in the hallway, partially disguised by the thick dust and low light in the building. Puddles of blood mixed with dirt next to the dead. There were holes in the roof and Mark could see a clear, starry night above them.

They moved toward their ammo bunker to get more ordnance and were joined shortly by others doing the same. The reinforced room was a mess from the bombardment. Most of its contents lay haphazardly, but they were able to find what they needed.

"Everyone have night vision?" Valentine asked as he made sure a monocular worked before attaching it to his helmet.

"Don't skimp on the ammo," another said.

"I heard they're inside the wire," someone added.

"Did they cut through the fence like last time?" Val asked.

"I don't know, but they're everywhere. I barely made it here. Bastion was hit, too. They took out the fuel dumps and aircraft blew up in massive fireballs."

"Are you boys ready?" Mark asked.

"Bekommen einige!" Hans yelled in roughly perfect unison with his new partner.

The others yelled their own motivations as they left, but Mark agreed with Hans and Dieter. "Get some!"

Not knowing exactly what they would encounter, they moved swift and silent. The sirens screamed from each corner of the base, alerting inhabitants of the attack. The group moved out together to assess the threat. All had their game faces on as they left the building. They stacked up near a concrete wall surrounding the buildings, put in place as a protective barrier against attacks such as these. Part of the wall exploded as a mortar round detonated. The explosion killed two men and the concussion knocked most of them down.

Gunfire flashed far and near as they assessed the situation.

"We need to find out where the attack is coming from," Mark told the remaining men, once they were back on their feet.

"They appear to be everywhere," Val said.

"Who are they?" another asked.

"Follow me and choose your targets. The enemy is mixed in with friendly forces," Mark told them. "Bounding overwatch, people."

They moved out in a staggered leapfrog formation toward the base's perimeter while viewing the horrific scene in front of them. Wounded men and women were staggering and crawling, some screaming for help. Targets were acquired along the way, but not all were engaged.

"Who's who?" Hans yelled.

"Left flank!" said another. Most stopped, took a knee or dropped to the ground and fired multiple rounds at few people in Afghan dress shooting at them with AK-47s. One of the insurgents exploded. The shockwave took Mark's breath away. He recovered and stood up, momentarily dazed and confused.

"Let's move, people!" Valentine commanded.

A bright flare popped above, illuminating the area like a supernova had exploded. Bullets zipped past them and hit what remained of the buildings.

"Incoming!" Dieter yelled as the man next to him took a bullet.

"Muzzle flashes on the right," Mark said turning to engage.

"We need to find a secure area and defend it," they all geard over the radio in their earbuds.

They moved into the shadows to avoid being detected, while still advancing toward the perimeter. Most of the living they encountered were wounded and dazed, but some were combat ready and were enlisted to help defend the base with the others already moving to contact.

Flares continued to illuminate the surrounding area and muzzle flashes were seen nearly everywhere.

Mark caught sight of a familiar figure. "Hephzibah!"

"What's happening?" she asked once she reached Mark and the others.

"I don't know, but it looks like the enemy is inside and outside the base. Grab that rifle and stay close. We're going to repel them from the perimeter on this side."

Hephzibah grabbed an M4 lying next to a body. She took extra magazines from the vest pouches and caught up to Mark.

The growing group reached the outlaying buildings of the camp. Mortars were firing off in the distance past the fence with low thumping heard after the flashes of light from the rounds leaving the tubes.

"Snipers, take those mortar crews out!" Hans yelled as he started to engage through the night vision scope on his rifle.

Two pop-up flares were ignited and set sailing over the fence farther down the perimeter. They burst over the desert floor and the light showed a large force making its way to the base's fence.

"Everyone disperse so we look like a larger force," Mark said.

"Light 'em up, don't let 'em get to the fence!" a voice screamed.

"We need air support," Mark heard over the radio.

"Does anyone have comms with any of the air stations?" Valentine asked.

No one had radio contact with aircraft in the area. An endless wall of lead was thrown at them from all sides. Several men were hit.

"There's more coming from the left flank!" Someone warned.

Gunfire erupted louder, closer. The firefight kept building, becoming more desperate. Mark saw another man fall as a bullet found him and tore through his flesh.

*How long can we keep this up?* Mark wondered.

A fusillade of fire erupted behind them as machineguns opened up in long, deafening bursts, like they were having a conversation.

Mark, Hans and others turned to engage.

"Do you boys need some assistance?" called a familiar voice from the shadows, walking into the dim light around them.

Mark was glad to see Duke, Schnell and a handful of people in full combat gear standing by the crumbling concrete wall. They added to the defense of the fence line.

Duke had been watching Schnell while Mark had gone on missions. Schnell loved to assist in the pub, keeping the peace while Duke sold booze.

"Do you know who's attacking us?" Mark asked him, firing two quick rounds at a combatant running toward them.

"No idea, brother. But I do know that, whoever they are, they're inside the base as well as well as out there. They hit the command and communications centers along with the flight line with suicide bombers. I heard they detonated themselves in most of the troop barracks, too. I saw one of the little bastards vaporize right in front of me when he was shot. The vest must've been packed with a massive amount of explosives. It killed a good deal of people around him."

"All we have is comms with each other," Mark told Duke. "We need air support, but no one has a radio able to transmit long range."

"Let me see what I can do. Sanchez, Rios come here."

Another flare popped and illuminated the area in front of them. Shadows rippled across the sand and were fired upon by some obviously nervous troops.

A thunderous noise began swelling in front of them, growing louder as the seconds passed. Another flare popped over the desert, exposing what lay in wait. The sand in front of the perimeter fence came to life as black-clad figures lurched forward, spitting flame from AKs and PKMs fired from the hip. They were still a few hundred meters away but closing the gap with speed.

"I hear something," said a voice over the radio. "It sounds like an aircraft inbound."

Mark threw an IR strobe over the fence as far as he could and told anyone else with one to do the same. "With any luck, the pilot will see the strobe and realize we're marking a target."

"Get a radio so we can talk to those pilots," Duke ordered.

"We're on it, boss," two men said as they disappeared into the shadows with haste.

"Incoming!" someone yelled. Mortar rounds hit a building nearby.

"Do they know where we are?" another asked.

"If they don't, they might get lucky," Mark said.

Mortar and RPG rounds sporadically hit near them while they continued to engage the threat.

Suddenly, two A-10 Thunderbolts flew side-by-side low over the area. The Warthogs — so called because they're old and ugly but extremely effective — pulled up once they started taking fire, but quickly circled back around. A few men stood up and cheered, quickly ducking back down as one of them was hit by an incoming bullet.

"Take out those targets to the north," Hans radioed.

"I've got 'em!" someone said, firing a machinegun from the roof of an adjacent building.

"Here they come," someone yelled as the Hogs came back around.

Along with the tracer fire on the ground, the sky in front of the two aircraft opened up like flame shooting from the mouths of dragons. Their 30-mm GAU-8 Avenger rotary nose-cannons threw devastation down to Earth. The two second *BRRRRRRRRRRTT* burst was deafening but much appreciated by the people defending the wall. The cannons on the aircraft chewed up the insurgents and sand on the other side of the fence with the depleted-uranium rounds. Dust and smoke enveloped the enemy forces who were still heading toward the base.

The birds finished the strafing run and peeled off to start another. Mortars continued to fire in the distance, pounding buildings and the ground inside the base. The first aircraft made another pass along the perimeter while the other moved out to attack the mortar crews in the distance with AGM-65 air-to-surface missiles. The explosions were brilliant, lighting up the horizon and illuminating more of the desert and the invaders. Secondary explosions could also be seen. Mark, Hans and the others were having a hard time seeing targets through the thick layer of smoke hanging stagnantly above the sand.

The two aircraft left the area after making eight runs on the enemy.

"They must've expended their ordnance and needed to rearm," Mark said as he dropped an empty magazine and inserted a loaded one into his rifle, then closed the bolt.

"I'm running low on ammo," Hans said as an explosion blew a hole in the perimeter fence.

"Contact front!" Dieter yelled. He started shooting and moving forward as another flare popped overhead and machineguns chattered back and forth, far and near.

"Dieter!" Hans roared.

A few seconds of silence followed, as if everyone in the fight stopped shooting or changed magazines at once. Mark saw Hans open mouth but heard nothing. Then suddenly, hell was again unleashed upon the Earth.

# Chapter Thirty-Seven
**Camp Leatherneck,**
**North Eastern Perimeter**
**Sunday, October 19th 0252 Hours**

Flames seemed to erupt from the night as rifle barrels flashed and spat lead. Greatly outnumbered, Mark and the others still conceded no ground.

Dieter was hit multiple times in his legs, arms and face. Hans pulled him to cover, but he was gone.

Duke fought beside Mark, both men taken off guard by the mass of men pouring through the hole in the fence, shooting in their direction. Two men lying next to the broken concrete wall opened up on the insurgents with SAW machineguns. Tracer fire from the belt-fed weapons packed the hole with an unyielding barrage of bullets as the dead enemy combatants piled up, filling the void.

Enemy fighters were coming out of the shadows now, screaming and yelling "Allah Akbar!" The fight turned pointblank and hand to hand.

"God be praised' my ass! You can die for your God, Mohammed!" someone said from Mark's left.

Blood soaked the ground. It smelled like a slaughter house in the middle of a heat wave. The scene looked horrific. Defenders answered the enemy's praises to their god with obscenities, which were, at times, unrecognizable.

One man lay nearby curled up in a fetal ball; his eyes wide open, fixed in place, body frozen with fear, unable to fight any longer. He shuddered as explosions rocked the vicinity.

Mark and Duke heard a loud crash behind them. They pointed their rifles at the source of the noise, then smiled and lowered their weapons.

"I found a Prick 150," Sanchez said standing up from the deck.

"What the hell did you do, trip?" Duke asked him. "And where's Rios?"

"I think I've been shot in the leg, and Rios didn't make it. A fucking haji ran right into him and pulled his ripcord. Poor guy didn't even have time to react. They both vaporized in front of me and painted the nearby walls red. The blast blew me back 20 feet. I thought I was a goner, too."

"Damn! OK, get on the radio and get us more air support and reinforcements."

"Forthwith," Mark added. The men stared at him. "It's something Happy would say if he were here. Stop staring at me and just do it, Marine."

"Roger that," Sanchez said.

Muzzle flashes and the continuous popping of gunfire continued as the dwindling group fought back against the seemingly never-ending enemy force.

"Mark, get down!" Duke yelled, tackling him.

They fell to the ground as a muzzle flashed multiple times right next to them. Sand flew around them. "Duke!" Mark rolled the man off him and caught his breath.

Schnell growled and grabbed a woman's arm, pulling her into the illuminated area as a flare popped overhead.

"You bitch!" Duke coughed up blood and gasped for air.

Hans stepped into view and fired his sidearm. A single bullet hit the woman in her forehead. Her head snapped back and blood splattered under the glow from above. Schnell let go of her arm. Hephzibah fell to her knees and toppled over, lifeless.

"Hephzibah!" Mark yelled. He looked from her to Duke and Hans.

"He's gone," Hans said. He stood over Mark, blood trickling down his left arm and dripping from his fingertips.

"What the fuck? Why did you...?"

"Did she hit you?"

"I don't believe. Yeah, I took a couple rounds in my front SAPI plate. And this," Mark showed Hans the hole in his right shoulder. "Are you sure she was aiming for me?"

"Without question, brother," the large German said. "Schnell confirmed it."

"I was with her last night! Why would she...?" Mark was confused. "She looked like a stone-cold killer."

"She sure did. I'm sorry, bro."

"Choppers!" someone yelled. The birds flew low over the men moments later.

The four Apache helicopters fired their nose cannons and rockets at the incoming enemy forces, then were gone.

Two -10 Warthogs took the helicopters' place and flew low and fast right above the base. They pulled up and banked left after surveying the scene below. The aircraft circled around for another pass, and this time lit up the area outside the perimeter with their cannons. *BRRRRRRRTTTTTTT* drowned out much of the rest of the battle until they finished their gun run.

The battle started to die down.

"Sanchez, are you talking to them?" Mark asked.

"Roger that, sir."

"Tell them to concentrate their fire to the north. Do we have reinforcements coming?"

"Troops are inbound."

"Did you tell them the enemy is mixed in with friendly forces?"

Sanchez gave Mark a thumbs-up as he keyed the handset. "Roger that, Outlaw Two Six. Be advised, we have haji's in the wire. I say again, the enemy is mixed in with friendly forces inside the base."

Mark heard a muffled voice from the earpiece as Sanchez continued to talk to the pilots.

From the dark desert floor, a rocket fired and tracked the bird on the right. Counter measure flares lit up the sky behind the Warthog and the rocket exploded, narrowly missing the aircraft.

Mark scanned beyond the perimeter where he saw the rocket leave the ground. "I see where it came from, Engaging now." He shot nine rounds at multiple targets and felt the bolt lock back on the empty magazine. "Changing!"

A Marine staggered by Mark and Sanchez minutes later. He dragged his rifle in the sand with his right hand, his left arm hanging limp, leaving a trail of blood. "Is it over?"

"Somebody grab him," Mark said. "He's in shock."

The popping of gunfire continued sporadically but slowly died down to an eerie calm in between. The occasional explosion was heard in the distance. The enemy wasn't breaking contact to regroup and counterattack. They had finally been extinguished, crushed and defeated. Pockets of resistance were still fighting, but they wouldn't last long.

"Hans, are you still good to go?" Mark asked.

"Ja."

"OK, friendly troops are en route to track down remaining enemy combatants. When the cavalry arrives, they won't know who to shoot at."

"What do you suggest?"

"How about the Dungeon?" someone suggested.

"I heard that's how they got on base to begin with," another said.

"Then it's exactly where we need to go, for both reasons," Mark said, "Let's go! Schnell, 'hozzam'."

She followed Mark.

# Chapter Thirty-Eight
Baltimore, Maryland
Top floor of the Executive
Security Building
Saturday, October 18th, 1606 Hours
Local Time

"Sir."

"What is it, Danni? I was about to leave."

"Mr. Ryland is on line three and says it's urgent."

Tom pushed a button, "This had better be good Dennis! I have a party to attend at the White House."

"Go Packers."

Tom sighed and secured the line by pushing a button and flipping a switch. "We're good, what is it?"

"We've had a base incursion on Camps Leatherneck and Bastion."

"How bad?" Tom asked. He sat back down.

"Catastrophic, I'm sorry to say. We lost contact with all of our assets in the first few minutes of the engagement. They were blindsided. The enemy hit

Leatherneck and Bastion simultaneously from inside and out. I've tried contacting everyone we have there, but no one is picking up."

Tom grabbed the remote, turned on the TV and clicked through the channels. "I don't see anything about it on the news."

"Because it started less than 10 minutes ago."

"How did we find out so quickly?"

"I was on the phone with the Admiral when it started. Before the line died, I heard gunfire and explosions."

"What were you talking with him about?"

"We believe someone hacked into our mainframe and accessed classified documents."

"You didn't consider it pertinent to tell me?"

"I was only informed a short time ago and you were in a meeting. I was going to speak with you, then this happened."

"All right. Call the Pentagon and offer our full support. Start rerouting all available personnel to the region. I want updates as it progress, on both fronts. Make sure we have plausible deniability. Cover our collective asses, Dennis."

"That's what I get paid the big bucks for, boss."

"Pack your bags. I want you in theatre ASAP." Tom hung up the phone. His cell-phone buzzed to signal a text message. He didn't recognize the number.

*Unknown - Turn on the news*
*T. King - Who is this?*
*Unknown - A friend*

Tom turned the TV back on and turned to a news channel. The White House press secretary stood behind the podium. "A few minutes after 2 a.m., local time, U.S. Camp Leatherneck and adjoining British Camp Bastion came under heavy insurgent attack from a still unknown force. We don't know the extent the damage or loss of life. The other U.S. bases in the region have been put on high alert and combat-ready units have been deployed to both camps under attack. We will keep you informed as new information comes in. Thank you."

The room erupted in a frenzy of questions, but no answers were given. Tom turned off the TV and pushed the intercom on his desk phone.

"Yes, Mr. King."

"Danni, can you call the White House and confirm whether or not the dinner is still going to happen."

"Right away, sir."

His cell buzzed again. It was the same number from before.

*Unknown - Damage control time?*

*T. King - Who the hell is this?*

*Unknown - I already told you, a friend*

*Unknown - The whirlwind is about to start*

*T. King - I have nothing to hide*

*Unknown – We both know that's not true, Tom. Enjoy your evening at the White House*

"Son of a bitch!" Tom yelled.

# Chapter Thirty-Nine
## The Dungeon
### Sunday, October 19th, 0437 Hours

"No go! No go!" Mark yelled as he turned back, bullets zipping by and raking the concrete and wood around them, sending splinters and dust into the air. "Schnell, heel! I mean, la'bhoz."

"Those sound like AKs to me. I can take a few guys and flank them," Hans said. He quickly peered around the corner at the burned-out Humvees from which they were taking fire.

"Sounds good. Take two men around the building and let me know when you get close. We'll open up and you frag the shit out of 'em."

"Got it."

The three men slipped into the darkness at the rear of the building as Mark looked back at the rag-tag team. "Bring your SAW up here."

A man moved passed the others and stood next to Mark.

"I have a full can, sir," the Marine said.

"All right. Watch the corner. I'll be right back," Mark whispered.

"Roger that."

"Valentine," Mark said, looking behind them. No one answered. "Did anyone see what happened to Val?" His question was unanswered. "Damn it!"

Two minutes later, Hans's voice came across the radio in Mark's ear, "We're set."

"Standby," Mark said.

Mark and the Marine with the machinegun fired relentlessly at the vehicles. Return fire rocked the building next to them until four explosions lit up the area from which the enemy fire had come.

"All clear," Hans said after the dust cleared.

"We're coming to you," Mark replied.

Mark, Schnell and the others met up with Hans and his team. The destroyed Humvees were so marked with bullet divots, scars and missing paint they looked like they'd been in the target area of a rifle range. The dead insurgents wore U.S. Army-issue uniforms but had chest rigs for AK-47 magazines.

"I don't like the look of this," Mark said to Hans.

"Make sure of your targets before you pull the trigger," Hans said to the group.

Faces showed horror as they realized the enemy looked almost exactly like them. Mark took the lead with Schnell as they moved toward their destination. Moments later, more gunfire erupted.

"Those sound like an M4s," someone said.

"Let's see." Hans peeked around.

A bullet hit the corner of the wall nearby. "Friendly!" Mark yelled as more flashes of gunfire rang out.

"Friendly! U.S. Marines, damn you!"

"All clear! Come on over," a voice yelled back.

Mark slowly looked around the corner through his night vision monocular. Two figures were standing by a crippled Humvee. "Coming over. Don't shoot!"

Mark's group made its way to the vehicle and the two men.

"Who are you?" one of them asked.

"Marines and civilian contractors. We're headed to the Dungeon. Troops from the surrounding bases are headed here and it's about to get even uglier. Friendly fire is gonna be everywhere."

"Can we go with you?"

"Follow us and keep your finger off the trigger."

The group had grown to 10 people as it moved closer to the barracks, where they came under fire once more. They looked for cover but there wasn't much.

"Cease fire, damn you!" Mark yelled at the troops inside the building. "We are friendly!"

"OK! Sorry! Come on in," someone inside shouted back.

"Mark," Hans said.

"Yeah."

"We lost another three."

Mark looked back at the bodies. "Damn! Let's get inside."

"Grab their grenades and ammo," Hans told the last two men in the group. The Marines hesitated for a moment, then did as Hans instructed.

Single file, the remaining men moved into the building. Schnell followed directly behind Mark. Various parts of the structure were caved in and she stopped and sniffed several times.

"Hey. Sorry, but I thought you were the hajis coming back," a Marine told Mark.

"Sorry is all you have to say? You just killed three Americans!" Mark slammed the man into the wall. Schnell growled and moved closer.

"Take it easy," Hans said. "It could've happened to any of us."

"You're with us now," Mark said. "You better be sure who you have in your sights before you pull the trigger again."

"Yes sir!"

"This would be a good time to dress our wounds," Mark told Hans. "If anyone's been hurt, get over here. The rest of you fan out and cover us."

Wounds were assessed and wrapped with gauze and tape. It would have to do until they found a corpsman.

Mark and Schnell led the group through the maze of broken-down concrete walls and ceiling. "What happened in here? Was it from the mortar attack?"

"Maybe part of it, but most of the damage was from one of those suicide fuckers," one of the Marines said.

"They came in when we were sleeping and this is what happened," another added.

"All right, Mark said. "The stairs look to be intact. Follow me one at a time and keep your fingers off the trigger. I don't want to get shot in the back."

Mark activated an IR flashlight so he could see in conjunction with his night vision monocular, as did anyone with the same devices. Darkness enveloped them as they descended the three flights of stairs. Some of the group could see nothing and held on to those who could. They started seeing bodies as they rounded another corner on the second sublevel. Most were American but others were dressed in black. Some of those still had bomb vests on.

Mark stopped at the bottom. "I see lights up ahead," he whispered.

They rounded another corner. "I thought you saw lights?" Sanchez whispered back.

"They were right there."

Muzzle flashes lit up the corridor from the spot Mark indicated, and the sound of gunfire slammed against their eardrums. Bullets tore into the rock on their left. Shrapnel flew everywhere as the copper and lead broke apart on the limestone. Fragments hit some of them.

"U.S. Marines," one of Mark's group yelled out.

The attackers were silent for a moment. Then, "How do I know you're not the enemy?"

"Do I sound like a damn terrorist?"

"Not really."

"Then don't shoot us. We came down here to help."

Mark and his men turned off their night vision and lit the hallway with weapon lights and flashlights. Three men down the corridor did the same and came out from behind a makeshift barrier of desks, chairs and mattresses.

"Who are you guys?" one of them asked.

"Yeah, are you the cavalry?" another wanted to know.

"It's still pretty bad upstairs," Mark told them. "We came down here as reinforcements began to arrive, for shelter and because we heard this is where they infiltrated the base to begin with."

"What, are you afraid to stay and fight?"

"Afraid? Hell no! But friendly fire is going to kill countless more Americans before this is sorted out Devil Dog. If this is where the enemy entered, then we're going to plug the hole. Now, do you want to stay here and hide, or do you want to come with us and kill these bastards?"

"With you. We were getting bored here anyway."

The other two nodded their heads in agreement.

The now-larger group moved out with Mark and Schnell in front. Mark stayed calm, cool and completely purposeful, even though he'd been wounded. More bodies of the enemy forces and Marines lined the tunnels. They were checked, but none were found alive until Mark rounded a bend and ran into the business end of an M4. The wounded Marine pulled the trigger, but the bolt had been locked half open and an expended case stuck out of the ejection port.

"Easy, buddy, we're the good guys," Mark told him as he pushed the muzzle down.

"They were everywhere! We didn't stand a chance," the Marine said. His eyes were bloodshot and pinned open, looking around franticly.

"Where are you hit?"

"Hey, Mr. Dog," the Marine said as Schnell moved close and sniffed him.

The man showed Mark his leg and pointed at his chest.

"I'm going to wrap these and come back for you."

"NO. Take me with you."

The man dug his fingers into Mark's arms, despair and doubt on his face. Tears welled up in his eyes, but he held back their release with all his might.

"We can't, but we'll be back. We need to find out how they were able to get inside so quickly."

"The right spur, they came from there. Dozens of them. The wall just collapsed and they poured inside. There were *so* many of them."

"OK. We *will* be back for you."

The group continued. They saw more carnage the farther they traveled.

"Let's go in here," Mark said.

"The guy back there said the insurgents entered farther down the passageway," Sanchez said.

"I know some of the guys in here. Maybe they can help us or shed some light on what happened."

"Did someone let one go?" someone asked from the rear as they cautiously entered the room.

"No, you smell sulfur, composition C and death," Mark said.

It was dark as sin inside the room. An eerie silence permeated the cavern as the group moved forward.

"It looks like a bomb blew up in here," Hans whispered as they shined weapon lights around, illuminating body parts and splashes of crimson and charred wood. Parts of the room had caved in.

"The walls look like that paint-splatter artist," someone whispered. "What's his name?"

"Pollock I think," another said.

"Jackson Pollock. Yeah. It does look like he was here," Sanchez agreed.

"I hear something," Mark announced. He held a fist into the air and the rest of them stopped. He motioned for them to take a knee while he investigated.

The room had been the command office for Executive Security. The steel door was creased and partially blown off its hinges.

"Memphis," Mark called softly.

No reply. He moved the door enough to slip through. It creaked loudly. Two bodies lay face down inside. Mark rolled them over and recognized one as Nate. Blood and shell casings littered the floor. Mark heard movement by a desk that had fallen on its side and was covered with bullet holes.

"Memphis?"

"Who's there?"

"It's Mark Mitchell."

Mark moved slowly, shining his light. Memphis lay behind the desk in a pool of blood. He'd been shot multiple times. A rifle lay next to him with the bolt open and no magazine in the mag well. He barely clutched his handgun, the slide locked open.

"We gave them hell, but they...There was too many of them." He coughed up thick, bubbly red plasma.

"Take it easy, buddy. I'll get you a corpsman down here."

"I'm done, Mitchell, but I can try to make amends."

"What do you mean?"

"This flash drive will give you your answers. We're the reason the base was. I was only following orders. I had no idea why they were."

"Stay with me. What do you mean? Who is 'we'?"

"I thought we were doing it for our country...Tell my wife I love her, and I'm sorry."

"You can tell her yourself. What's on this memory stick?"

"Everything you need to shut them down. Be careful who you trust Mitchell. Don't...don't trust Col. Ja..."

He slipped into nothingness and was gone.

Mark's mind raced. *What the hell was Memphis talking about?*

"Mitchell," Hans said. "We have movement coming down the corridor. Is anyone alive in there?"

"Not anymore," Mark said. He slipped the drive into his pocket. "What do we have?"

"We're not sure, but it's coming from the breach in the wall."

"Look alive, people," Mark said. "It's about to get real."

They moved into the corridor and positioned themselves on both sides, some standing and others kneeling for a clear line of sight. The quiet corridor filled with the shadows of what headed their way.

"Contact front!" someone warned.

"OH MY GOD!" Another yelled.

The deafening sound of gunfire filled the void as muzzle flashes from both sides lit the confined space like fire fountains from a volcano.

Mark looked at Hans and they both had the same idea. "Frag out," Mark yelled as they both tossed grenades. "Schnell, move!"

# Chapter Forty
## Troop Barracks, above the Catacombs
### Sunday, October 19th, 0642 Hours

"Sound off! How many made it?" Mark asked as they rushed up the steps, nearing the surface.

"There are four behind me. Two more fell farther behind with the wounded Marine from earlier," Hans said. He coughed and shook his head. Dust fell from his hair.

"How did we not die?" Sanchez asked, breathless, as he reached the top of the stairs, his limp becoming more pronounced.

"The blast wave from the suicide vests sealed the tunnel. If we hadn't have been running at the time, we'd be buried along with them," Mark said.

"I don't remember seeing so many haji's in the same place," one of the Marines gasped.

"I can't go any farther," another said as he limped to a stop and sat down. "I think some of your grenade is in me."

"If it wasn't for my grenade, you wouldn't be here to complain," Mark snapped.

"I hear choppers," Hans said while they looked through the rubble of the barracks. Light shown through openings in the ceiling and walls.

"I'll take this guy and we'll find a safe evac route," Mark said, pointing at a dirt-covered Marine. "Hans, keep her here, will ya? Schnell, ma rad."

"Don't worry, she'll stay here, won't you, girl?" Hans patted her side, knocking dust off her coat. He spoke to her in German and petted her as Mark left.

Mark and the Marine made their way through the rubble toward an opening. The bright sunlight blinded them. Squinting, they moved closer. Burnt gunpowder and explosive residue filled their noses. U.S. troops were abundant outside, with helicopters flying overhead continually.

"People are everywhere. It's over!" the Marine shouted, attempting to go outside.

Mark grabbed him, "You need to be careful. I'm sure there's a good number of itchy trigger fingers out there. "Go slow with your hands up. Do what they say and tell them you're a Marine or you might get shot."

"Roger that, thanks!"

"I'll go back to the group and tell them help is on the way, I need you to bring help to us."

"It's on the way."

Mark watched the Marine slip out of the crack in the rubble and make contact with a group of soldiers. They pointed their rifles and ordered him to the ground, as Mark predicted they would. Mark started back to the others but heard a noise in another part of the barracks and went to investigate.

It looked like a meeting room. Part of the roof had caved in but appeared mainly intact. He saw nothing immediately. Suddenly, something took him down hard from his right side. They fell to the floor, sliding and came to a stop where pillars of light shown through the roof like spotlights. The attacker, jumped up and disappeared. Mark pulled himself up and looked around.

"Who's there?" Mark yelled, shining his light, but seeing nothing.

"It's over, Mitchell," a deep voice said from the darkness.

Mark pointed his rifle and light in the direction of the voice. "What's over?"

"You are, boy!"

Snake walked into the middle of the room with two machetes. He slid one across the floor to Mark and started spinning his around like a sword.

"Are you serious?" Mark asked him. "Haven't we been through enough this morning?"

"Pick it up Mitchell!" Snake barked. A wicked, sinister grin formed on his face. "Only one of us is walking out of here alive."

Reluctantly, Mark took off his helmet, tactical vest and unhooked his drop leg holster. His body armor and remaining loaded magazines would only slow him down.

Snake took off his t-shirt and collected his long hair into a ponytail. As soon as Mark picked the machete up, Snake attacked. The blade sliced, making a *swish* sound as the air was displaced by the sharp edge.

"This is for Jigsaw, you son of a bitch!"

The blades connected with such force that sparks flew. They swung the machetes as if they had trained with them for years. Both incorporated kicks and punches. Some connected and others were blocked. It was only a matter of time before one was the victor, and one was dead.

Mark landed a solid kick to Snake's chest, which threw him back across the concrete floor. The man rolled and came up crouching, flexing his bulging muscles. They both huffed, using the reprieve to catch their breath.

"Out of curiosity, why the nicknames?" Mark asked, half taunting Snake.

"We earned them!" Snake yelled as he commenced another attack.

Snake had roughly 50 pounds and four inches of reach on Mark. Mark knew he had to keep his distance and try to wear the man down, especially since he'd already been wounded.

"But, why do they call you Snake?"

"Because I crush my enemies! Stop talking and fight!"

Snake played right into Mark's plan.

The steel on the large blades continued to make contact and echoed through the otherwise silent room.

Snake sliced the machete through the air, making Mark move farther back. Their blades connected once more, and Snake pushed hard. They were toe to toe, face to face. Snake pulled away slightly and brought his weapon downward, slicing down Mark's right bicep.

Hurt, but not done, Mark feigned a more serious injury. This drew Snake in. He let Snake hit his machete a few times and let him knock it out of his hand. The blade slid across the room, coming to rest with a thud against a wall.

Snake tossed his machete as well and approached Mark, who held his arm with blood dripping from his fingertips.

"You're going to suffer now, boy."

"I was doing my job," Mark said. "I didn't know who I had in my crosshairs."

"It don't matter none. You took Jigsaw's life, and now I'm going to take yours. Simple as that."

Snake closed in, his arms reaching for Mark's neck. Mark attacked like a king cobra fighting a mongoose. He was the snake now, as he flicked the hand of his hurt arm. Blood splattered on Snake's face as he swung at Mark.

Mark blocked the large arms and kicked Snake hard in the groin. It sounded like his pelvis shattered. The sound echoed in the room. A couple of palm and elbow strikes to Snake's head and jaw, then a round kick to Snake's left knee sent him to the floor. Mark pulled some wires off a damaged section of the wall and tied Snake's hands behind his back.

"Tell me what you and your company were up to!" Mark demanded.

"I'll never talk!" Snake spit a mouthful of crimson blood at Mark.

"Pretty much what they all say, at first."

Mark punched Snake repeatedly until he heard ribs cracking and breaking.

"What you were doing! What did Memphis die protecting?"

"Never," Snake wheezed and winced in pain.

Mark grabbed the man's right hand and broke his thumb. Snake tried to yell, but his broken ribs stopped him. Snake looked white as a sheet, on the verge of passing out from the pain. Mark knew he was out of time and produced his Benchmade pocket knife. He punctured Snake's trousers near his lower right thigh with the tip of the blade and sliced his pants open to his waist.

"Now, which one of your family jewels would you like to keep?" Mark asked.

"I'm going to kill you, Mitchell!"

Suddenly, lights flashed on in the room. "Stop! Drop the knife or we'll open fire!" a voice called.

# Chapter Forty-One
**Remnants of Camp Leatherneck**
**Sunday, October 19th, 0723 Hours**

Mark and Snake were dragged outside into the debris-littered sand. The sun was blinding, making it impossible to see who stood above them. From the ground, Mark could see clean boots and Army combat uniforms.

"I'm Lt. Sandusky, 10th Mountain Division. And who are you men?" asked a short, thin man.

"I work for Executive Security and you have no authority over me, boy!" Snake wheezed.

"I don't care who you say you work for. Until I can identify you, you're an enemy combatant. And who might you be?" Sandusky asked Mark.

Mark squinted upward. His eyes were finally adjusting and he could see the man. Mark's mind was delirious as he spoke. "Snake's right, you do look like a little Army boy."

Snake started laughing and Mark followed suit, not even knowing why.

"Why were you fighting?" Sandusky asked.

The laughter continued. Some of the soldiers tried to hide their grins.

"Cuff this one and take them both away!" the lieutenant growled.

Mark knew it didn't matter who they said they were. The soldiers could see they were Americans, but until they were processed and verified, they would be treated like the enemy. It would get sorted out quick enough and he would be on his way.

Bodies, weapons and gear were being staged around them as they were escorted to a makeshift triage area in a field where Mark had played baseball a few times. EOD teams and bomb-sniffing dogs were abundant. They were busy checking the numerous brown spots of spilled blood and the craters left from enemy mortar rounds. There were a few enemy soldiers in one area, while the other held Marines, sailors and other Americans.

"What do we have here?" a portly Army first sergeant asked the soldiers as they walked up with Mark and Snake.

"Two smart-asses," a sergeant said. "This one with the long hair says he works for Executive Security, and this one hasn't said anything yet. He was trying to kill the big guy here and might've succeeded if we hadn't broken it up."

"Who are you?" the first sergeant asked.

"I'm Mark Mitchell and I'm attached to the base's antiterrorism task force. I report directly to Col. John..."

"Colonel!"

Mark saw Col. James walking toward them.

"Is this guy one of yours?"

"He is. I'll take it from here, soldier, cut these ties off this man's wrists."

"I'll see you later," Mark told Snake.

Snake smiled and satt more blood at him. Two soldiers restrained Snake and walked away with him.

"Mitchell," Col. James said. "Have you seen anyone else from the task force?"

"The only one I know is still alive is Hans Richter.

"Where's is he?"

"He was with a group of Marines in the troop barracks. I'm sure he'll be along shortly."

"I know this isn't how we planned it, but since they came to us, it made it much easier to defeat them."

"But if we had taken the fight to them, we wouldn't have sustained the amount of causalities we did."

"I agree, but it is what it is."

"How did you fare? You don't have a scratch on you," Mark said with a condescending tone, not liking how James spoke.

"I was in the command center when the base was attacked. With the concrete barriers surrounding it, it was the safest place to be. A large number of our troops fell back to the security of the structure and helped fortify it. The insurgents hit it hard, but they didn't get far. Only sections of the building were damaged."

"What about the med center? Did Happy make it?"

"I haven't been there yet, but I was told it was well defended against the enemy forces. You should head over. You look like you need medical attention anyway."

Mark looked at his bloodied and ripped clothing, caked dirt clinging to a few places.

"As Hans would say, they're just scratches."

"Scratches or not, you need to get them looked at. Come find me at the command center later."

"Roger that."

Mark made his way to the medical center. The scene inside was chaos.

"Excuse me?" Mark said to a young Navy petty officer.

"What can I do for you private?"

Mark laughed. "It's major actually, petty officer. And I need medical attention."

She stood at attention and noticed Mark's battered appearance. "I'm so sorry, sir. I didn't see any rank on your collars."

"I must've lost them in the battle this morning."

"Yes, sir! Right this way, sir. What's your name?"

"Mark Mitchell."

"I'll retrieve your records as soon as I get you on a bed, sir."

She took Mark back to the triage area. She talked briefly to a Navy commander and briskly left the room.

"So where did you get hit, major?" the commander asked.

"I only want to get bandaged up and get out of here."

"I see. Where are your wounds then?"

"I was shot in my right shoulder and took some grenade shrapnel to both legs."

"Let's get your clothes off and take a look."

"Commander, here are this man's records," the petty officer said minutes later, carrying a folder.

"Thanks, darlin'," Mark said with a slanted grin, laying on the gurney in nothing but his smiley-face boxers as a Navy nurse started cleaning him up.

The nurse finished attending to his numerous wounds and the doctor came back with a tiny bottle and a syringe.

"I don't need it, Doc," Mark told him. "Save it for other patients."

"You're going to want a local while I take out some of these chunks of steel and sew them up."

"I'm serious Doc. I'm good to go. You can check my records, but I shouldn't I need a tetanus shot, either."

"Please verify that," he said to the nurse as he handed her Mark's records. "OK, Mr. Mitchell, here we go."

The commander dug into Mark's left leg, pulling out pieces of a fragmentation grenade. They sprayed saline on each area before, during and after each fragment was taken out. Mark winced as a large chunk was removed from his upper right thigh. The bullet wound on his right shoulder was a through-and-through and was easily cleaned up.

"What did this?" the commander asked about the long gash on Mark's right bicep.

"It was a machete and it's a long story."

"It looks fresh, When did it happen?"

"After the battle was over this morning. Like I said, it's a long story."

The commander shook his head. "Well, Mark, I'm actually impressed. I don't remember ever having a patient with this amount of wounds not want any painkillers or be completely sedated. Well, there have been a few Navy SEALs, but none this bad as far as I can remember. Will you at least take these antibiotics, or should I keep these for someone else too?"

"I'll take those," Mark said and got dressed.

"I would recommend a change of clothes, but I wouldn't shower until tomorrow. Change your bandages as needed. You need to take it easy for the next couple of weeks so you don't tear any of those stitches loose."

"Roger that. Thanks Doc."

Mark slowly made his way out of the building, limping and with his right arm in a sling. He stopped by the room Happy had been in, but found no one there. "Excuse me," he said to the petty officer at the front.

"You again?

"A friend of mine was in a room, but now he's gone. Can you tell me what happened to him?"

"We transferred several people to Kandahar this morning."

"He was in a coma with a head injury and I was told he shouldn't be moved."

"Oh, yeah, that guy. He woke up this morning and was sent to Kandahar for sure. I signed him out myself."

"Thanks, darlin'," Mark winked and left her staring a hole in his back.

Mark slowly walked back to what remained of his barracks. It looked like a ghost town inside the building, not the normal blaring music and people milling about.

"Anyone home?" he asked as loud as he could muster.

No response.

Mark was about to his room when he heard, "Who's there?"

"Hans, is that you?"

"Mitchell! I thought you left us," Hans said as he walked down the hallway from the locker room.

"I was on my way back and got into a tussle with one of those Executive Security guys, then we both got detained."

"Yeah, they came in for us, too. I'm just glad we both made it, brother." Hans bear-hugged Mark, but stopped when he heard a grunt of pain.

"Where's Schnell?"

"The soldiers tried to take her, then they tried to shoot her when she growled at them, but I wasn't going to let either of those happen. She's in your room. I was coming back to bring her some food and water."

Mark opened his door and Schnell came to his side. She nuzzled and licked his right hand, but quickly stopped as Hans set the food and water down.

"I'm sure she's starving," Mark said. "Thanks for bringing it to her."

"She's a fellow soldier. I would do it for any one of us."

"Who else from the task force made it?"

"Besides us, I believe only Valentine, but we won't know for sure for awhile. It's a mess out there."

"It sure is," Mark agreed.

"I'll let you relax. See you soon."

"Thanks, brother."

"Don't mention it. Oh, and I found your rifle and gear," Hans pointed at the right corner by Mark's TV.

"Thanks again."

Hans left and Mark slowly undressed and put on some loose gym clothes. Schnell could sense his pain and whined when she next approached him. Mark sat on his bed. He held his face in his hands exhaling loudly. When he inhaled, his breath shaky, he felt tears running down his face. Wiping his eyes with the back of his hand, he grabbed his laptop and turned it on reaching for the memory stick Memphis had given him. Moments later, he entered his password and the home screen popped up with a picture of him, his son Michael and his ex-wife Sara at Huntington Beach when they vacationed in California. It was the year before Michael's accident.

Mark pulled the flash drive from his pocket and plugged it in. A window opened. He clicked on the 'open folder to view files' option. Only one folder named 'ES' came into view. He clicked on it and started reading and clicking on different files in the folder.

A few minutes later, Mark woke a sleeping Schnell when he yelled, "You sons of bitches!"

# Chapter Forty-Two
## Camp Leatherneck Command Center
## Monday, October 20<sup>th</sup>, 0948 Hours

"I still don't understand why I've been called here," Col. James argued with a broad-chested Marine major outside Gen. Moore's office.

"I still have men and weapons unaccounted for and I need to."

"It will all be explained to you shortly, Colonel," the major said, cutting him off. "Please take a seat and Gen. Moore will be with you as soon as possible."

Being one of the only structures on the base that stood nearly 100 persent intact, the command center had become home to more personnel than ever before. The offices and cubicles were saturated with men and women in uniform. Conversation filled the air like a stock broker's office floor on Wall Street. The power was back on for some sections of the base and land lines for the phone system were being restored. Crews had been up throughout the night getting vital components back in place.

Statistics reported that the loss of life for one single battle hadn't been this staggering since the battle of Khe Sanh in 1968. Not counting the enemy forces, hundreds of coalition forces and civilians had been killed, hundreds more wounded and a staggering amount were still unaccounted for from both bases. Many would never be found, as a result of the devastation the suicide bombers inflicted. It would be days, if not weeks, before the total numbers finally came in and next of kin were given a clear answer as to the fate of their loved ones.

The military bases in the country had been put on high alert. Smaller outposts and FOBs were being reinforced as much as possible. More combat units, some who had only been home for a short time, were being remobilized for duty in Afghanistan.

The web was full of recently posted videos from numerous organizations congratulating Al Qaeda, the Taliban and Pakistani militant groups, mostly made up of Sunni Muslims, for the attack. Most Western countries raised their terror threat levels not long after the story was released, for fear of more attacks.

The base commander of Leatherneck, Major Gen. Ronald Moore, had assumed command of I Marine Expeditionary Force a year prior and had been doing an exemplary job. He stood tall and lean, pushing 6'5" and was especially intimidating because of it. His salt-and-pepper hair showed not only his age, but his experience.

The base's security had been at the level it should have been. The men and women who had been on guard the morning of the attack were not at fault. They were simply taken by surprise and overwhelmed. The attack would be under investigation for months if it wasn't for new information recently brought to light.

"Gentlemen, will you please come in?" the major spoke to the four men including Col. James, waiting outside the conference room.

Gen. Moore and Mark Mitchell were standing at a long table.

"Thank you all for coming," Moore said, adjusting his glasses. "Please be seated."

"What's this about?" a man in a tailored suit asked.

"Mr. Smith, or whoever you really are," the general began. "This base was attacked a little over 24 hours ago by highly trained men and women, hell bent on killing every last one of us. Can any of you tell me why and how they were able to do it?"

The four men looked at each other and around the room. Heads shook. "I suppose they surprised us," a British officer spoke up.

"Captain, did you hit your head yesterday?" Moore asked.

The Brit touched the bandage on his forehead "Well, I did get..."

"That was a rhetorical question, you idiot! Of course they surprised us."

"Mitchell, why are you here?" Col. James asked.

"That's an awfully good question, Col.," Moore said, twisting his class ring from officer candidate school. "Mr. Mitchell, one of the *incredibly* brave men who put his life on the line to defend this post, has brought me some extremely disturbing, dare I say, damning information. Some could even say its very nature is nuclear in substance."

"I don't understand, general."

"Well, I'll give you a short synopsis of what's on a memory stick that has been brought to my attention. It's especially intriguing, to say the least."

"I told you general, if we were playing poker, we could clean house," Mark said.

"Are you men OK?" Moore asked. "Most of you look like you've seen a ghost, and I haven't even begun."

"I don't have to listen to this," Smith said, standing up.

The three doors to the room opened and heavily armed MPs burst in, pointing their weapons at the four men. "You *will* sit down and you *will* listen!" Gen. Moore ordered.

Smith sat back in his seat.

"From men and women in uniform on this base to internal members of the U.S. government, as well as a civilian contract company known as Executive Security who *had* incredibly lucrative contracts in countless parts of the world, I'm literally disgusted to find out the level of involvement each of you had in this," Gen Moore said.

"What do you mean had?" asked a man dressed as a contractor.

"Mr. Ryland, I will not be interrupted again," Gen. Moore instructed. "The men and women mentioned here have committed treason, as far as I'm concerned."

"I still don't understand what this has to do with me," Col. James said.

"Well, 'Admiral,' as you're called in certain circles," Moore said, "I saw you've been double dipping And I *will* have the next person who interrupts me, gagged."

James' face sank as he looked around the room.

"That's right, Mr. James, you've been caught red-handed," the general said.

"Hand in the cookie jar, maybe?" Mark added with a smirk.

"Sounds about right," Moore nodded and the major opened a door for a man in a suit who stood on the other side. "Gentlemen, this is Matthew Laughlin. He is with the State Department and was extremely interested to hear this information. Mr. Laughlin has already started the ball rolling up the chain of command. Arrests are being made around the world by law enforcement agencies. This is truly another sad day for America."

"You have no idea what you're doing!" Dennis Ryland yelled. "The stability in this region will implode without us here. The work being done behind the scenes is fragile, at best. If you do this, you're condemning all of us! More attacks will be carried out across the globe and they will make 9/11 look like a stroll in the park. I'm begging you, don't do this!"

"Captain, gag that man," Moore instructed. "Now that it's quiet again, to answer the initial question. The reason for the base attack was payback. Chatter has confirmed three — count my fingers gentlemen — three highly pissed-off terror organizations banded together for this holy war. It was highly coordinated and extremely well funded. How did they do it? The internal attack came from the catacombs under the base. They dug under the fence and came out in the Dungeon. Mr. Mitchell and the men and women who so valiantly fought beside him, several of whom gave their lives, thwarted a second attack that was meant to take out the first responders."

Gen. Moore continued listing evidence found on the flash drive. The four men in the room were about to be taken into custody when Smith, from the CIA, pulled a tiny hideout revolver and put it to his temple. Without a word, he pulled the trigger. Blood, skull and brain matter were plastered all over Ryland and a Marine lance corporal was hit in the arm with the rest of the bullet after it passed through Smith's head. His lifeless body fell out of the chair.

"Marines, take the rest of these men away and search them more thoroughly than they were the first time," Moore instructed.

On behalf of Executive Security, Memphis and his men had made a deal with the Mujahedeen "Freedom Fighters" of the Panjshir Valley region. They would provide weapons to the locals in return for large amounts of the precious gem being mined there. The weapons and ammo came from U.S. stockpiles paid for by American taxpayers, which cost Executive Security nothing. The stones were transported across the border to Pakistan where they boarded planes headed to the States and Europe. There, the raw materials were cut and processed for sale worldwide. All of this had been documented and backed up by corporate files.

Executive Security used the bulk of the money from the sale of the emeralds for anonymous political donations worldwide and helped fund illegal black and covert operations overseas, as well in America. Shell companies were set up to make the contributions. They were legit companies that did real consulting work or sold real products, but the money from the emeralds had been carefully laundered through them and dispersed where they needed it.

Coups were organized, dictators were put in power, civil wars started, and Executive Security sent in advisors or full-blown heavy hitters to make sure there were smooth transitions. With the private protection, the rest of the world would hopefully stay out of the way. With the deep pockets and ties the company had within the U.S. government, more than a few operations were sanctioned when they normally would not have been. The rest of the money generated from the sale of the gems funded countless, still unknown agendas.

Emeralds are smaller and lighter than gold, which makes it an easier commodity to transport and sell. Once cut, the stones are worth thousands, sometimes tens of thousands of dollars for only one karat.

Memphis and most of his men were dead. The ones who were left weren't talking. A range of top players, including board members of Executive Security were in the wind.

"It's a damn shame what happened to Duke," Moore said as he and Mark finished cigars in Moor's office.

"Yes, sir," Mark agreed. "He didn't deserve to go out like he did."

"No. no, he didn't. I served with Major Thompson on more than a few occasions. He had always been a stellar Marine and will be greatly missed."

"He surely will, sir."

"Hans Richter told me Duke saved your life."

"He did, and so did Hans."

"It's hard to believe a highly decorated soldier like Hephzibah Romach was merely a paid assassin. I met her when she arrived here. I didn't see it coming."

"I was as blown away as you were, sir, nearly literally, in fact."

"This is going to be another black eye for America."

"General, what if Dennis Ryland's claims of destabilization are true? I mean, look what happened when only three organizations commingled."

"You bring up a very good question, and I was wondering, what are your future plans?"

"What did you have in mind?"

"A new anti-terrorism task force is being formed and will be run out of Kandahar Air Base. They could use a man of your caliber."

"I actually thought about retiring, sir."

"Men like us don't retire Mitchell, we simply accept the next mission. If you do this, you have my full support, 100 percent."

"I will consider it, general."

"You can take as long as you need. I've read your service record and I have to tell you, I'm thoroughly impressed. You will make a great addition, wherever you go."

"Thank you, sir."

"However, I don't understand why you left the Corps after 16 years and achieving the rank of E-7, in the infantry no doubt."

"I had my reasons General."

"I'm sure you did. Please let me know your answer is about the task force."

"I will, sir, and I hope my report is detailed enough."

"I'm sure it will be Gunny. Thank you for your service, Marine."

Mark shook the general's hand and said, "Semper Fi," which the general reciprocated.

Mark slowly started back to his barracks, thinking of his next move.

# Chapter Forty-Three
**Baltimore, Maryland**
**Top Floor of the Executive**
**Security Building**
**Monday, October 20th, 0816 Hours**
**Local Time**

"Danni, I need you to get Dennis on the phone ASAP."

"Right away, Mr. King."

It had been a long weekend and Tom started to get settled at his desk when his office doors burst open. Men and women in suits and black jackets rushed in, pointing rifles, shotguns and handguns.

"Mr. King, I tried to stop them, but they say they have a warrant," Danni called from behind the intruders.

"What's this about?" Tom demanded.

"Thomas King, you're under arrest for espionage, federal weapons, conspiracy and terrorism charges," a tall, thin man in a dark suit and bulletproof vest said as he approached the desk.

"I beg your pardon! Who the hell do you think you are?"

"We're the FBI, Mr. King. I'm Special Agent Stanly Buchannan, and I've been waiting years to do this. Cuff him, men. And, someone read him his Miranda rights. "

"Hold it right there," a commanding voice said from the back of the group of agents as they handcuffed Tom.

"Who the hell are you?" the FBI agent asked the pudgy man with glasses and a bad haircut, who pushed his way into the room.

"I'm Nelson Baldwin, and I'm Mr. King's attorney. I have in my hand an injunction from District Court judge Harold Shumaker by way of the U.S. Attorney General's office. You can seize computers and documents in the building, but you cannot arrest Thomas King or anyone else listed on your warrant."

"This is ridicules," the FBI agent said, then looked at the paper. "Damn it! Take the cuffs off."

"How the hell did you get this injunction so fast? We received the warrant less than an hour ago."

"I'm told that's classified," Nelson told the agent as he wiped beads of sweat from his brow with a white cloth.

"Nelson, what the hell is going on?" Tom wanted to know as he was released.

"Agent Buchannan, we will be in the conference room if you need Mr. King for anything. Come with me, Tom," Nelson said, still out of breath.

"Mr. King, I have the information you wanted me to get," Danni said, rushing to keep up with Tom and Nelson as they walked briskly to the conference room.

"Follow us, please," King said.

The door closed and Danni looked at Nelson, then back to King.

"Whatever you have to say, darlin', I'm sure it's nothing I don't already know," Nelson said.

"Go ahead," Tom told her. "He has clearance."

"Sir, the entire network is being torn down. Mr. Ryland has been arrested in Afghanistan and Executive Security personnel are being detained and questioned at all locations, not only in CONUS, but worldwide."

"Talk to me, Nelson. How bad is it?"

"She's right, Tom. This is worse than bad. The State Department has given the feds more latitude with this than I've seen in a very long time. Someone is head-hunting here, and heads will roll."

"But we were working with the State Department, the joint chiefs and, hell, the president himself gave us the green light on numerous operations. Why this, why now?"

"The attack on Camps Leatherneck and Bastion. Right now I've stopped them from taking action where you're concerned. But it could go the other way, and fast. If enough evidence is brought to light, you could be indicted on all the charges the warrant stated."

"Please tell me this isn't happening!"

# Chapter Forty-Four
**Kandahar Air Base**
**Friday, October 24th, 1026 Hours**

Mark and Schnell were visiting Happy in the medical treatment facility on a hot and slightly overcast morning.

"How you doing, brother?" Mark asked.

"Doc says I'm going to make it, but I won't be dancing for awhile."

"Glad to hear it. You shouldn't dance anyway, you're terrible at it."

"Funny guy aren't ya? I hear I slept through one hell of a battle on Leatherneck."

"You did. We lost a lot of good men and women. I wish I'd had you by my side out there, but I hear you were well protected."

"Suicide bombers, I heard? I also heard you were instrumental in stopping the second wave that would've taken out the first responders."

"Right place, right time, I suppose. Nothing left to say about it. Besides, I wasn't alone. Schnell, Hans and several others were right there with me."

"You know if you were still on active duty they would've awarded you the CMH, right?"

"Maybe, but I'm just glad I was able to help."

"But, the medal of honor would've been the icing on the cake. You could write your own ticket with it."

"You know that isn't why I do it."

"Recognition isn't why any of us do it, brother, but sometimes it helps, right?"

"The base commander had a hand in my next duty station and it comes with some perks."

"So you're leaving me again? I actually thought you might retire after this. It's not like you need the money."

"Retiring was my first thought, but I took a job right here flying helo's and doing work on base. After a well-needed vacation at home in Alaska. We fly out this afternoon, and Schnell gets to come with me."

"Sounds like a dream job. I wish I could go to Alaska with you. Is Schnell ready for retirement?"

"It's better than getting shot at, and pays the same. Get better and you can come visit me and I know she's going to be plenty happy."

"Sounds good. What made you decide to stay?"

"Let's just say Gen. Moore reminded me why we do what we do. Besides, I'm getting too old for the grunt stuff."

"Don't give me that shit!" Happy told him with a slanted grin. "You have a few good years left in you. I'm the one who needs to retire."

"Yes you do, old man. How long are they keeping you here?"

"A couple more days here and it's off to Germany and then to Walter Reed. The doc said I shouldn't do anything too strenuous for a couple of months at least."

"You be nice to the nurses now. Don't do anything I wouldn't do."

"You can count on it, 'cause I know there isn't much you wouldn't do," Happy said.

Mark shook hands with his brother in arms before leaving the room.

"See ya soon, brother," Happy. as cheerfully as he could.

The nerve damage in his face from the bullet ricochet made his speech slurred. Mark could understand him where others couldn't.

Mark had a few more hours to kill before his flight to Germany and then on to the states, so he stopped by and visited with a few colleagues. A priority on his list would be one person who wouldn't be very happy to see him. Their history was a love/hate type of thing. Their professionalism moved to the front when it had to, but anyone who didn't know better would assume they were either married or divorced.

"Well hello Victoria," Mark said as he walked into the lounge workers were converting into the command center for the new counter-terrorism task force.

She turned around, and as her long hair caught up with her body, her smile slowly dissipated when she saw who said her name.

"I can see this is going to be a long tour, or are you lost? I can get you a service animal. Oh wait, I see you already have one. You two make a great couple."

"Oh, come on now, baby. There's no reason to be rude."

"Don't call me that!"

"Yes, ma'am. What would you like me to call you then, *sweetheart*?"

"Mark, I'm busy. What are you doing here?"

"I simply wanted to stop and say, hellooo."

"Somehow, I doubt it."

"I just came from visiting my buddy at the hospital and I wanted to see where I'd be working, and I knew you were here," Mark smirked.

"I'm busy, Mark."

"Too busy for me?"

"All kidding and past transgressions aside, Mark. You did a great job on Leatherneck," Victoria said hoping to change the subject.

"What past transgressions? You're the one who didn't want to continue what we had going."

"You can't be serious for even 30 seconds can you?"

Mark winked. "I remember when I made you smile and laugh so much your face hurt."

"I grew up. If all you want to do is reminisce, I don't have the time or patience right now.

"There was something crucial. Now, what was I going to ask you?"

"Mark!"

"Oh yeah. I have a list of items I'll require during my stay. I was told you can procure them," Mark said taking the paper out of his pocket.

She took the list and started to read it. "Are you joking? A putting green? Pink flamingoes for your Feng Shui?"

"Damn. sorry, those don't belong there," he said, taking the paper, scratching and writing in another place. "The flamingos go with the wading pool and tower sprinkler. I'll need to be near a water source, also."

"A picnic table and a Traeger?"

"Oh and can you add some folding chairs? Maybe ten? You never know when company might show up."

"Are you serious? A Traeger?"

"All right, I'll settle for a lesser grill if I have to, but do your best, will ya?"

"This is ridicules. It would be much easier to get you machineguns and explosives than what's on this list. Besides, I don't believe I have to."

"You do. Take a look at my orders."

"Where do you expect me to get a trailer? Why can't you live in the barracks with the rest of the men?"

"I was offered this posting with the understanding that each of my needs would be met. Who's in charge of the task force? Should I go talk to him instead?"

"His name's Major Johnson, and no. I can handle this, but I can't promise all of it."

"Are you jerking me around with his name? I hope for his sake he makes lieutenant colonel soon," Mark's laugh rang in the empty room.

"I'd be careful, Mark. I hear he's a real badass," she said, hiding a grin.

"I'll keep it in mind, darlin'. I'll see you in three weeks."

"Take your time coming back."

"I know your heart went pitter patter when you saw me. We'll have to catch up when I return."

"It's going to stay professional."

"I'll need the entire list when I get back in three weeks. It's really nice to see you again Victoria."

Victoria glared at him and walked away.

"She never did like being called anything other than her name," Mark mumbled to Schnell as he made his way out of the building.

The flight to Germany was quick since Mark had slept the whole way.

"How long are we going to be here?" Mark asked one of the crew as the plane taxied after landing.

"Less than an hour. We need to refuel and take on a few more people," an airman told him.

"Do you mind if we stretch our legs?"

"Be quick about it. I'm sure this one needs to do his business."

Schnell growled at the airman and Mark corrected him, laughing. "Yes, I'm sure she does."

Not long after they made it back on board the aircraft's power plants started back up and they were rolling down the runway. Mark and Schnell would be flying the military hop from Ramstein Air Force base to Elmendorf in Anchorage, and then on to Eielson in Fairbanks. The trip would take about 20 hours. Mark would be home for three weeks before heading back to Afghanistan.

He planned on making the best of his R and R, though his main priority before having any fun was finding someone suitable to watch Schnell once he left. He needed to find the perfect fit for them both. There would be no way he would leave her in a kennel for as long as he would be gone. This new contract was for a year, and he wanted her well cared for.

Schnell fell asleep not long after takeoff. Mark followed suit not long after, thinking of home.

# Chapter Forty-Five
## Alaska
### Saturday, October 25th, 1119 Hours

The C-17 Globemaster military transport touching down on the landing strip at Elmendorf Air Force Base woke Mark from a sound sleep. He lifted the brim of his Barrett hat, yawned and stretched while looking out a tiny window next to him.

"We're finally back in America, girl," he told Schnell, who let out a low moan as if answering him. "Look, what's all that white stuff?"

The crew chief walked through the cabin and reminded the dozen passengers to wait to disembark the plane until the honor guard carried off the two flag-draped coffins in the back. A Marine and a soldier; were returning home.

Once they were allowed off the transport, Mark grabbed his carry-on and he and Schnell walked through the ankle-deep crust to the nearest hangar. She ran around barking and playing in the snow like it was her first time. Mark was sure it wasn't, but thought it great she played like a puppy.

He saw the Anchorage skyline over the base. Low-lying clouds hung slightly above the tall buildings but still allowed a view of the majestic, snow-capped mountains of the Chugiak and Kenai ranges to be seen.

The wait for their flight to Fairbanks would be a couple hours. Mark had no other luggage, so he didn't need to wait for anything. A television was on in the hangar with a couple of airmen watching it. Thomas King, founder and CEO of Executive Security, sat at a long table in a large room in front of a Congressional oversight committee. He was there to answer for his company's involvement regarding alleged illegal activity at home and abroad.

"Can you believe this guy?" one of the airmen said as he turned up the volume.

"They say he and his mercenaries are the reason for the base attack last week," another airman added.

"I hope every last one of them gets fried!"

A camera panned the room showing the panel of old men up front. Another angle showed a gallery of onlookers and camera flashes from the numerous reporters in the back. A man in the middle of the panel called the session to order and Tom King started talking.

*"Chairman Kennedy, congressman and other members of the committee. My name is Thomas King. I am the chairman and CEO of Executive Security. My company offers military*

*and law enforcement veterans of our fine country a way for them to continue to serve after separation from their previous duties. We form teams of dedicated personnel and send them where they are needed, to protect Americans and their interests worldwide. My words cannot express the respect I..."*

"I, for one, have heard enough of this man's political bullshit," Mark said, as he and Schnell walked away. Several men and women with whom he had served had died because of the monster on TV. And he tried to say he did what he did for his country? Mark knew there would be a special place in hell for men like Tom King.

"He'll get his, girl," Mark whispered to Schnell as he found a coffee maker in a corner by some offices.

"Does your dog have a leash?" an airman asked while Mark poured a cup.

"No, she doesn't, but she doesn't need one."

"She does if she's going to be in my hangar."

"All right," Mark relented. "Would you happen to have something I can use?"

"I might have some paracord in the office."

"That will do."

Mark took the cord from the senior airman and attached it to Schnell's collar. He whispered in her ear as she whined. "This is only temporary, girl. When we get on the next flight, I'll take it off."

The flight from Elmendorf Air Force Base to Eielson was a little bumpy as the C-130 flew over the Alaska Range but smoothed out the closer they got to Fairbanks.

"That's Denali," Mark told Schnell as they looked out one of the little windows.

"Are you going home, sir, or passing through?" an airman asked as Mark walked by.

"We're just taking a little R and R from Afghanistan. We have a home in Fairbanks."

"Were you there when Camp Leatherneck was attacked the other day?"

"Yes we were, weren't we, girl?" Mark said rubbing Schnell's ears.

"I heard it was a hell of a battle. I'd love to meet the guy they say stopped the second invasion while the first responders were there."

"It sure was a hell of a battle."

Mark and Schnell sat back down. He knew the man was only trying to make conversation, but Mark didn't want to relive the moment. It happened, he remembered, and as far as he was concerned, he wasn't a hero.

Mark tried to doze off again but had already slept enough and the coffee in Anchorage had rejuvenated him.

The short flight from Anchorage to Fairbanks was nearly over as the crew walked through the belly of the aircraft, checked the cargo in the middle-rear once more and made sure the occupants were seated and secure. Even though there were only six passengers on board besides the crew, the pilot came across the intercom and gave a weather synopsis and welcome home speech.

"You're going to love your new home, girl," Mark told Schnell as the plane landed on the airstrip at Eielson and taxied to the nearby hangars.

"Where are you transferring from?" an Air Force captain sitting nearby asked.

"We arrived from Kandahar today."

"That's one hell of a weather change."

"About a 60-degree difference. At least it's 16 above and not subzero here right now."

"Too true. What branch are you in?"

"Civilian, actually," Mark said as they disembarked. "It's been nice chatting with you, captain."

Mark and Schnell walked to the nearest hangar and found an airman who would take them to the Post Exchange where he could call a taxi. The ride to town would take about 45 minutes. Mark called and gave the company instructions on where to meet him, then went inside to get a burger and fries.

A woman sweeping the floor paused to protest. "You can't bring your dog in here," she said.

"Schnell is a military service dog, ma'am. We won't be here long. You won't even know she's here."

Schnell simply sat beside Mark and sniffed. She offered no challenging reactions. She had only growled at one person since they left the Middle East.

"Uh huh. We'll see about that."

A half an hour later, two military policemen approached Mark and Schnell as they were leaving the burger joint.

"Can I see some ID, sir?"

"Is there a problem here, guys?"

"We received a report of a man with a dog causing problems. You do know only service animals are allowed in here, right, Sgt. Mitchell?"

"It's gunnery sergeant and you can ask any one of these fine people. All we did was get some lunch. This is Schnell, and she is a combat veteran. So she is a service dog, boys."

"We're going to have to ask both of you to leave, sir."

"Airman, we're merely waiting for a cab ride into town. It should be here shortly. Would you mind if we wait near the entrance, but inside?"

"That would be fine, but keep her on a leash."

"Roger that."

"Where you headed?" the cabbie asked, taking off his cap and rubbing his bald head.

"It's the corner of Hilton and Wilbur."

"You betcha. You and your dog recently fly in from somewhere?"

"Afghanistan."

"It's pretty crazy over there right now, huh?" The driver turned on Flight Line Avenue and headed for Hursey Gate and the Richardson Highway, then into town.

"It sure is."

"Were you there for the base attack?"

"We were and we heard all about it."

Mark steered the small talk to the weather.

"I heard a storm front's moving in and it's supposed to dump a couple feet of snow," the driver said.

The scintillating conversation broke off when the driver received a call on his cell-phone. Must be his wife, Mark figured, from what he could overhear of the nagging on the other end. More power to her, as the call lasted most of the rest of the ride, leaving Mark to sit back and take in the winter scenery.

As they moved closer to town and Mark could see Fort Wainwright, the Army base, off to their right, Mac hung up the phone.

"I'm real sorry about the call mister, the dish washer broke again."

"It's all good," Mark told Mac.

The taxi finally turned on to Hilton Avenue and Mark took in the familiar surroundings. They pulled up to the duplex Mark owned and he could see his neighbor's VW Jetta in the other driveway.

"It looks like Christie's home," Mark told Schnell, then opened the door.

Schnell ran around the snow-covered yard with the paracord attached to her collar, trailing her every move. Mark paid the driver and walked up the steps. He unlocked the door and called Schnell, who came instantly. They walked inside and Mark started to pull the door shut when a hand stopped it.

"Who the hell are you?" a man's voice said, bearing a hint of authority.

Mark opened the door back as Schnell started growling at a tall scruffy-looking young man.

"I'm the guy who lives here," Mark told him. "Who the hell are you?"

*Schnell's judgment is sound,* Mark thought. *I'd better continuing listening to her. This guy looks suspicious.*

"Mark, is that you?" a soft voice came from behind the man on the porch.

"Hey Christie. Did I forget to let you know I was coming back?"

"Yes, you did," Christie said, but had seen Schnell. "But it will be just fine if you tell me who this little lady is."

"Christie, meet Schnell."

"Schnell! What a lovely name. Where did you come from?" she asked, instantly smitten with the dog.

"I rescued her. She's a former military working dog, but recently retired. Christie, who's this?" Mark asked about.

"Oh, Mark, I'm so sorry. This is Tom. We have a few classes together and we're getting ready to head to our study group."

"It's good to meet you, Tom," Mark said, extending his hand.

Mark shook Tom's hand with a little more force than was necessary.

"What's wrong?" Christie asked.

"Nothing. Just a firm handshake, is all. Mark, what do you do for a living?" Tom asked.

"He's a business consultant," Christie offered.

"What kind of business?" Tom asked.

"All kinds," Mark replied.

Christie could sense tension and interrupted.

"Well, we'd better get going, Tom. We don't want to be late. Mark, I'll stop by and visit when we're done, if it's OK?"

"You're always welcome, darlin'."

"I'll see you soon, girl," Christie told Schnell, who sat panting heavily, her tongue hanging out of her mouth.

Mark and Schnell watched the petite strawberry blonde drive away. They went back inside.

"It appears we may have found the perfect person to watch you when I go back to work, girl," Mark told Schnell. She offered a low bark, as if agreeing with him.

The sun had set, but the sky above was illuminated with thousands of twinkling suns. The cold was a refreshing change from the stifling desert air. Neither of them could sleep, so they went back outside. Schnell frolicked around the winter wonderland of the tiny backyard. A flicker above caught Mark's trained eyes. A miniature light streaked across the northern heavens. Mark made a wish just as he and his son had on the rare occasion they would see a falling star.

He suddenly felt foolish. Michael was gone and this ritual should remain buried with him. But moments later, as if being answered by a celestial force, Mark's foreboding vanished as the aurora in its utter magnificence began dancing across the sky. Schnell nuzzled against Mark and he was content.

Special thanks to:

Jenny Neyman - For your detailed editing of my stories.

Joseph Robertia – For your continued support of my writing.

Monica Mullet – For helping make this character who he is.

Eric Cox – For your continued support and inspiration.

Sheila June Collins – For your continuing support and unwavering commitment.

Melanie Noblin – For taking my photos and turning them into art.

Tyler and Shane Larrow – Your contribution for the cover picture has helped bring Mark and Happy to life. Don't hesitate to let everyone know it's you in the ghillie suits behind the Barrett 82A1 .50 BMG and the FNH SCAR 17 .308. Thank you so much for taking the time and letting me take the 135 pictures of you on the mountain. You were Mark Mitchell and Happy for a day.

Afghanistan Combat Veteran, Operation Enduring Freedom 2012; Sgt. Jason Hale, sniper, Charlie Troop

1 – 126 CAV, Michigan Army National Guard – For reading this story and offering your advice and support. Your first hand knowledge as a military sniper in combat in the mountains of Afghanistan has greatly aided in the success of the character Mark Mitchell and this story. Thank you for your service to our fine country!

Joseph, Kyle, Monica, Amanda and Colleen for our writing club and for all the help and insight into my stories.

# About the Author

*Author Travis Wright was born and raised in a small, Oregon town, where his love of the outdoors began. He grew up hunting and fishing in the rural Northwest, a lifestyle that transferred easily to a life in the Last Frontier. Wright has lived in Alaska for 24 years and has recently retired from selling guns to write full time. He is enjoying a quieter life and has focused all of his time on storytelling for now. He is an NRA-certified instructor and continues to enjoy teaching others gun skill and safety, as well as shooting his own guns.*

*Wright's interest in firearm technology and his active duty service in the Marine Corps Infantry, are both influential in his work as a writer. While Wright has written poetry off and on for most of his adult life, his work as a novelist began in 2010 with the survival story, "Uncertain Times." Since putting that work to rest, he hasn't stopped writing. Wright's life-long active imagination and curiosity of the unknown have found their outlet in storytelling. The recent introduction of his fifth book, "The Wilderness" is sure to be a favorite.*

*Wright's current work, "Nomad," is the second installment of the "Mark Mitchell Chronicles," a prequel to the hit story, "DeadHorse." He looks forward to many more years of telling good stories, putting smiles on faces and keeping the pages turning.*